We believe a kid who reads is a kid who can succeed.

We believe it's every adult's responsibility to get books into kids' hands and into kids' lives.

We want to make reading fun for kids — through stories and voices that speak to them and expand their world.

We want to make books available to kids — through teacher scholarships, bookstore funding, school library support, and book donations.

We want every kid who finishes a Jimmy Book to say: "PLEASE GIVE ME ANOTHER BOOK."

Learn more about our initiatives at
JimmyPatterson.org

BOOKS BY JAMES PATTERSON FOR YOUNG READERS

THE TREASURE HUNTERS NOVELS

Treasure Hunters
(with Chris Grabenstein and Mark Shulman, illustrated by Juliana Neufeld)

Treasure Hunters: Danger Down the Nile
(with Chris Grabenstein, illustrated by Juliana Neufeld)

Treasure Hunters: Secret of the Forbidden City
(with Chris Grabenstein, illustrated by Juliana Neufeld)

THE MIDDLE SCHOOL NOVELS

Middle School, The Worst Years of My Life
(with Chris Tebbetts, illustrated by Laura Park)

Middle School: Get Me out of Here!
(with Chris Tebbetts, illustrated by Laura Park)

Middle School: Big, Fat Liar
(with Lisa Papademetriou, illustrated by Neil Swaab)

Middle School: How I Survived Bullies, Broccoli, and Snake Hill
(with Chris Tebbetts, illustrated by Laura Park)

Middle School: Ultimate Showdown
(with Julia Bergen, illustrated by Alec Longstreth)

Middle School: Save Rafe!
(with Chris Tebbetts, illustrated by Laura Park)

Middle School: Just My Rotten Luck
(with Chris Tebbetts, illustrated by Laura Park)

THE I FUNNY NOVELS

I Funny
(with Chris Grabenstein, illustrated by Laura Park)

I Even Funnier
(with Chris Grabenstein, illustrated by Laura Park)

I Totally Funniest
(with Chris Grabenstein, illustrated by Laura Park)

THE DANIEL X NOVELS

The Dangerous Days of Daniel X
(with Michael Ledwidge)

Watch the Skies
(with Ned Rust)

Demons and Druids
(with Adam Sadler)

Game Over
(with Ned Rust)

Armageddon
(with Chris Grabenstein)

Lights Out
(with Chris Grabenstein)

OTHER ILLUSTRATED NOVELS

House of Robots
(with Chris Grabenstein, illustrated by Juliana Neufeld)

Public School Superhero
(with Chris Tebbetts, illustrated by Cory Thomas)

Daniel X: Alien Hunter
(graphic novel; with Leopoldo Gout)

Daniel X: The Manga, Vols. 1–3
(with SeungHui Kye)

For previews of upcoming books in these series and other information, visit middleschoolbooks.com, ifunnybooks.com, and treasurehuntersbooks.com.

For more information about the author, visit jamespatterson.com.

TREASURE HUNTERS

SECRET OF THE FORBIDDEN CITY

BY JAMES PATTERSON
AND CHRIS GRABENSTEIN

ILLUSTRATED BY
JULIANA NEUFELD

LITTLE, BROWN AND COMPANY
NEW YORK BOSTON LONDON

Copyright © 2015 by James Patterson
Illustrations by Juliana Neufeld
Excerpt from *House of Robots: Robots Go Wild!* copyright © 2015 by James Patterson
Illustrations in excerpt by Juliana Neufeld
The JIMMY PATTERSON name and logo are trademarks of JBP Business LLC.

JimmyPatterson.org

Little, Brown and Company
Hachette Book Group
1290 Avenue of the Americas, New York, NY 10104
Visit us at littlebrown.com

Little, Brown and Company is a division of Hachette Book Group, Inc.
The Little, Brown name and logo are trademarks of Hachette Book Group, Inc.

The publisher is not responsible for websites (or their content) that are not owned by the publisher.

First Edition: September 2015

Library of Congress Cataloging-in-Publication Data

Patterson, James, 1947– author.
Secret of the Forbidden City / James Patterson and Chris Grabenstein ; illustrated by Juliana Neufeld. — First edition.
pages cm. — (Treasure hunters ; [3])
Summary: "The Kidd children—including twelve-year-old twins Rebecca and Bickford—follow mysterious clues that take them from China to Germany, in the hopes of finding their missing father and the treasure that will finally free their kidnapped mother"— Provided by publisher.
ISBN 978-0-316-28480-6 (hardcover) — ISBN 978-0-316-29986-2 (ebook) — ISBN 978-0-316-29987-9 (library edition ebook) [1. Adventure and adventurers—Fiction. 2. Buried treasure—Fiction. 3. Missing persons—Fiction. 4. Brothers and sisters—Fiction. 5. Twins—Fiction. 6. China—Fiction. 7. Germany—Fiction.] I. Grabenstein, Chris, author. II. Neufeld, Juliana, 1982– illustrator. III. Title.
PZ7.P27653Sec 2015
[Fic]—dc23

2014045235

10 9 8 7 6 5 4 3 2 1

RRD-C

Printed in the United States of America

THE WORLD
ACCORDING TO
THE KIDDS!

GREEN-LAND

NORTH AMERICA

THE UNITED STATES

EURO

NEW YORK CITY (NEW YORK)
WENT TO A "REAL" SCHOOL
HERE FOR THE FIRST TIME—
THAT DIDN'T LAST VERY LONG!

CHARLESTON (SOUTH CAROLINA)
THIS GENTEEL SOUTHERN
CITY HAS A SECRET BLACK
MARKET FOR ART—WHO KNEW?

ATLANTIC OCEAN

★ **MIDDLE OF NOWHERE**
WHERE DAD WAS LOST
FROM *The LOST*.

SOUTH AMERICA

BRAZIL

★ **RIO DE JANEIRO**
HAD THE BEST FRUITY
DRINK HERE—IT CAME
IN A COCONUT SHELL!

A

ASSORTED **BAD** GUYS. WE MEET A LOT OF THEM.

NOTE EXPANDING POOLS OF B.O.

MY TWIN BROTHER, ONCE AGAIN, FINDS HIMSELF IN AN AWKWARD POSITION.

NOTE SWEAT DRIBBLING UP HIS FOREHEAD. REGRETTING THAT EIGHTH SAUSAGE, ARE WE, BICK?

QUICK NOTE FROM BICKFORD KIDD

Okay, I'll make this fast because, as you can see, I look like I might hurl.

My twin sister, Rebecca, did that drawing of me being grilled by a criminal mastermind. In fact, Beck did *all* the drawings in this book. Wherever we go, no matter what happens, no matter how much treasure we find or how much danger her irreplaceable twin brother might be in, Beck keeps doodling in her sketchpad.

Meanwhile, I'm always scribbling in my handy-dandy spiral notebook.

Except when I'm upside down. Pens don't work upside down.

So that's the basic idea: I'm the writer; my twin sis is the illustrator.

This also explains why so many of her drawings have helpful notes like that one over there about my excess body odor. It's not really true. I bathe on a regular basis. Honest.

All right, already! Beck says I have to tell you that, sometimes, I make things up, too. In other words, don't believe everything you read or see. Adventures are like that.

You never know which way is up.

Especially when both your parents are CIA superspies and you're currently being tortured by being dangled upside down in a dungeon.

Yep. There's a lot to tell you about. Read on!

PART 1
YEAR
OF THE
BIRD

CHAPTER 1

We begin our tale of hunting treasure while avoiding torture in a very tight spot.

Literally.

The four of us—me; my twin, Beck; our genius sister, Storm; and our way cool older brother, Tommy—were being held captive by the notorious Dionysus Streckting, his sniveling minions, and their snarling dog, Munch—a German shepherd with a toxic case of beef jerky breath.

Streckting was seriously evil.

Everybody said so, including him.

"I am seriously evil, children. Pure, undiluted, one hundred percent evil!"

Storm, who has a photographic memory, not to mention an IQ somewhere in the stratosphere, had told us that Dionysus Streckting is considered the most nefarious, despicable, and just-plain-nasty criminal mastermind in all of Europe, including the island country of Cyprus, where a band of thugs had kidnapped our mom.

Streckting kept saying that if we helped him find a certain treasure map, he'd help set Mom free.

He'd also been dropping some pretty heavy hints that he knew something about what happened to our dad.

"Tell me where the map is and, perhaps, I may give you some valuable information my spies have collected about your father! Then again, maybe not. As I said, I am enormously evil."

It seemed as if my hunch could be correct: Dad hadn't been swept overboard when our treasure-hunting ship, *The Lost*, nearly capsized in a tropical storm off the coast of the Cayman Islands. He didn't drown or get devoured by sharks.

TAKE ME TO CHINA, CIA SPY HELICOPTER!

BICK MADE ME MAKE DAD SAY THAT. I STILL DON'T BELIEVE HE FLEW TO CHINA ON A SUPERSECRET SPY MISSION, EVEN IF BICK SAYS IT OVER AND OVER, WHICH HE DOES REPEATEDLY. STORM AND TOMMY DON'T BELIEVE IT EITHER. IN OTHER WORDS, THIS DRAWING WAS DONE ONLY TO HUMOR BICK.

Okay.

I wasn't absolutely, positively certain that Dad was alive and well and working undercover for the CIA. But Dionysus Streckting, the infamous criminal mastermind, was looking for him, too!

We couldn't *both* be wrong, could we?

CHAPTER 2

"Um, excuse me, Mr. Strepthroat?" said our big brother, Tailspin Tommy.

"Streckting! *Dionysus* Streckting. My mother liked grapes."

"Sorry. My bad. Anyway, could you untie us for a couple minutes? I haven't scrunched my hair in hours. Need to apply some product, pronto."

"*Nein!*" snarled one of Streckting's goons. (I got the feeling Streckting never did his own snarling; he paid people to snarl for him.)

"*Nein?*" said Tommy. "Is that German for *no*?"

"Yes!"

"Yes, I *can* go fix my hair?"

Streckting stepped forward. His boots creaked. "No one is going *anywhere* until one of you four children tells me everything I need to know."

"Fine," said Storm, who, like I told you, has a photographic memory. "You want me to start with the *A*'s? Aardvarks are…"

"Silence, *schreckliche Kinder*!" shouted the head German goon.

Munch growled and bared his glistening fangs. Tommy and Storm stopped yammering.

"Your father is not dead," hissed Streckting. "Would I be chasing him across two continents if he were dead?"

"Wait a second," said Beck. "How do you know our father is alive?"

"I don't. But I strongly suspect it."

Beck laughed. "Well, I strongly *suspect* you got that scar on your cheek from a kitty cat who didn't like you stomping on her tail, but I don't go around blabbing it to everybody, do I?"

"Silence! Where is it? Where is your father's treasure map?"

"Which one?" said Tommy, chuffing a laugh. "He had, like, a ton of them."

"They're stashed in safe-deposit boxes all over the globe," added Beck. "Asia. Africa. Europe. Not to mention New York, Chicago, and LA. Dad needed a key ring the size of a hula hoop."

"But then he fell overboard and died," said Storm, who can be kind of blunt.

"Enough!" said Streckting, raising a pistol with a very long muzzle. His minions raised their weapons, too. Munch, the German shepherd, probably would've done the same thing but he couldn't hold a pistol in his paws.

"You miserable children will tell me where your father, the great treasure hunter Professor Thomas Kidd, has hidden the information I so desperately seek or we shall shoot you. None of you will ever see your mother or your father again because you will all be dead!"

You know, maybe Beck was right.

Maybe we should start at the very beginning. I understand it's a very good place to start.

But, first, here's Beck with a sneak preview of coming attractions.

ALL THIS
AND MUCH, MUCH MORE!
COMING UP!
KEEP READING MY WRITING!

FINE.
Keep looking at Beck's drawings, too.

CHAPTER 3

Yep. It's been a busy few weeks for Kidd Family Treasure Hunters Inc.

And, this time, the treasure we're after isn't just for us.

Okay, finding Mom and Dad—*that's* for us. But the other loot? Well, let's say the number one rule of all treasure hunting, "finders keepers, losers weepers," won't apply this time.

Anyway, let's go back to the start of the story.

Happy times!

We'd just retrieved two superold (we're talking

centuries) Ming vases out of the cargo hold of a sunken treasure ship, one of the mammoth, nine-masted, quadruple-decked vessels from the fleet of Zheng He, a Chinese explorer way back during the early Ming Dynasty. In the fifteenth century, Zheng He made seven expeditionary voyages, sailing all the way from China to East Africa.

That's where we found the shipwreck—off the coast of Kenya.

Anyway, the Chinese Navy, assisted by our weird uncle Timothy (who was Dad's spy chief at the CIA, and who, I think, is a double or maybe triple agent), was right there in the Indian Ocean waiting for us when we surfaced with our two priceless artifacts.

Well, that's not completely true. The Ming vases do have a price. One had just been sold in Hong Kong for $21.6 million.

Go ahead. Do the math.

Yep. We're talking $43.2 million worth of pottery.

The Chinese government declared Zheng He's sunken ship (which was about the size of a mall) and all its contents to be a Chinese national treasure. That, of course, included the Ming vases we'd already hauled to the surface. So they were confiscated from us.

Total bummer.

And not because of the money. (Okay, a little because of the money.)

See, we needed one of the Ming vases to set our mother free.

And so we flew with Uncle Timothy and several assorted Chinese dignitaries to Beijing, hoping we could plead our case at the highest level. All we wanted was one vase.

No, we *needed* it.

Otherwise, we might never see our mom again.

CHAPTER 4

China is absolutely incredible.

Everywhere you look, new buildings are popping up. All sorts of creativity is being unleashed. The economy is booming. It's definitely a twenty-first-century superpower.

After a quick tour of Beijing, we were ushered in to meet China's high cultural minister.

There was a really cool painting of the Great Wall hanging on the Pretty Ordinary Wall of the minister's office. We brought the two vases and, in a brief ceremony, officially turned them over to the People's Republic of China.

"As you see, Mr. Minister," said Uncle Timothy, "anything you want, I can deliver. Anything. I look forward to our future cooperation as I pursue other cultural acquisition projects for our mutual benefit."

Everybody shook hands and bowed.

"Um, when you said 'I,'" Tommy whispered to Uncle Timothy, "you meant America. Right?"

"Oh, yes. Of course."

"Cool." Tommy started chanting and pumping his fist. "USA! USA!"

And everybody in the office stared at him.

Beck, who is our chief negotiator, stepped forward.

"Mr. High Cultural Minister, your exalted eminence, not to mention comrade of the people, sir."

A translator repeated all that in Mandarin.

"As you know, my brothers and sister and I are the ones who actually found the long-lost Zheng He treasure ship at the bottom of the Indian Ocean. We are also the ones who hauled those two barnacle-encrusted old flowerpots up from the deep."

"These are my nieces and nephews," Uncle Timothy added proudly. "Not really, but officially."

More translation. Lots of head bobbing.

Beck cleared her throat and shot Uncle T. a look.

"All we are asking for in return," she continued, "is that we be allowed to take one of those Ming vases—maybe one with the ugly dragon faces all over it—to some kidnappers in Cyprus, because we need it to barter for the release of our mother. Surely, sir, you understand. If your mother were being held captive by a gnarly group of scallywags, you'd want to set her free, too."

More translation.

"Uh-oh," muttered Storm, who understands Mandarin. "The translator just told the minister that you called his mother a gnarly, scallywag dragon face."

"But—but—" Beck stammered.

The high cultural minister held up his hand. Said something kind of brusque.

"We will think on this," said his translator.

"Thank you, Mr. Timothy, for bringing us this treasure."

"That's it?" Beck called after him. "You're not giving us the vase?"

"Not now," said the translator when the minister marched out the door. "But, to express our eternal gratitude, we will give you something much, much better!"

"But all we want—"

Before Beck could finish, a mob of people twirling ribbons flounced into the room followed by a group of synchronized dancers who had more moves than a marching band.

"We are very honored to present you with something much grander than a Ming vase," shouted the translator over the thundering drums. "Your very own *yóu xíng*!"

"What's that?" I asked, afraid it might mean *very loud traffic jam*.

"A government-sponsored, officially sanctioned parade!"

CHAPTER 5

Okay, I'll admit it—the Chinese definitely know how to throw a parade.

We were on a float—a miniature model of a Zheng He treasure ship—riding through Tiananmen Square in the heart of Beijing. The public square (the largest in the world) was filled with military bands and thousands of soldiers in crisp uniforms standing at attention, their eyes following us as we drifted past.

A government official led our parade. He stood with his head poking out of a limousine's sunroof so he could bark things into a bank of microphones mounted on top of the car. Every time he shouted, the soldiers shouted in reply.

"Tuōmǎsī! Lìbèikǎ! Dǎgōu!"

"They're chanting your names," reported Storm. "Thomas, Rebecca, and Tick."

"Tick?" I said.

Storm shrugged. "There's no Mandarin word for *Bick* or *Bickford*."

When the crowd shouted *"Sīdìfēnnī!,"* Storm's eyes turned as dark as a thunderhead. Yep. That's why Mom and Dad nicknamed her Storm.

"Stephanie?" she muttered. "Who told one point three-five-one billion people my real name?"

"Chillax," suggested Tommy, who was winking at every female ribbon twirler or fan flipper who glanced his way. As we neared the Tiananmen Gate (The Gate of Heavenly Peace), close to the Forbidden City, a million red balloons were let loose. A squadron of jets soared overhead to spray red, yellow, and white smoke trails.

It was like our very own Macy's Thanksgiving Day Parade. The only thing missing was a jumbo-sized Bart Simpson balloon.

It was awesome to have that many happy people cheering for us, even if they were butchering our names while munching on candied bugs. That's

right. In China, instead of hot dogs, the street ven-
dors sell skewered grasshoppers, grilled cicadas,
and deep-fried scorpions.

"Do vegetarians eat bugs?" asked Tommy,
scratching his head.

"No," I said. "Usually, it's the other way
around."

CHAPTER 6

As much fun as the parade was, none of us could forget the dark history of Tiananmen Square.

And, even if we could, Storm was there to remind us with her ready supply of tour-guide factoids.

"This is where, on June 3, 1989, Chinese college students gathered to demand free speech and economic justice. The students built a thirty-three-foot papier-mâché statue and called it the Goddess of Democracy, which kind of looked like our Statue of Liberty."

"Could you climb up to its crown?" asked Tommy.

Storm ignored him. "Then, of course, there was

the 'tank man,' who stood alone to block a column of tanks sent into the square to crush the protest."

If you ask me, that guy was the real hero of Tiananmen Square, but I bet the Chinese never gave him a parade.

"*Nǐ hǎo, měinǚ!*" Tommy shouted at all the Chinese girls, who were treating him like a rock star. "*Nǐ hǎo, měinǚ!*"

Storm rolled her eyes. "I never should've taught him that."

"What's it mean?" asked Beck.

"*Hello, beautiful.*"

While Tommy was flirting, I was wishing Mom and Dad could've seen our parade.

They would've been so proud.

The four of us had done pretty well since both our parents mysteriously disappeared. We'd followed in their footsteps. We'd discovered some awesome treasures and, best of all, when the going got tough, we always had one another's backs.

Mom and Dad had taught us a bunch of stuff when they homeschooled us aboard *The Lost*. We had read a ton of books, studied everything from math to martial arts, and learned how to take care of ourselves (yes, I'm talking laundry). But the most important lesson was pretty simple: Family comes first.

Family even outranks Chinese girlfriends. But, before our parade was over, Tommy had swapped contact information with about three dozen Beijing teenagers, including a pretty girl named Wang Xiu Ying.

"Her name means *elegant and brave*," said Tommy on the limo ride back to our hotel.

"Good," said Beck, "because she'd have to be brave to date *you*."

Since we were "Heroes of the People," the Chinese government put us up in a swanky, five-star hotel.

When we stepped out of our chauffeured car, Beck saw something across the street.

"Impossible," she muttered.

NOTICE HOW PEOPLE ON THE STREETS WEAR FACE MASKS? ↳

THAT'S **NOT** BECAUSE OF ALL THE SMOG IN BEIJING. IT'S 'CAUSE THEY HEARD B.O. BICK'S IN TOWN.

"What?" asked Tommy.

"It can't be."

"What can't be what?"

"Over there. The *Naked Woman on the Beach!*"

Tommy was definitely interested.

CHAPTER 7

Beck hurried through the bicycles, rickshaws, and motorcycles clogging the busy street.

"Where's the naked woman?" said Tommy, hurrying right behind her. "I don't see any beach, Beck!"

Storm and I were bringing up the rear as we hustled through the congested traffic.

"She's in the window right across the street," shouted Beck.

"Oh, man," said Tommy. "Naked women in windows? I love China!"

"It's a painting, Tommy," explained Beck, coming to a halt on the sidewalk in front of an art gallery.

My twin sis isn't just a great artist. She's also a
pretty amazing art historian.

Which, I guess, is why she made me look like
a cube head in that last picture.

"That's a woman?" said Tommy, staring at the
giant watercolor.

"Yes," said Beck. "Pablo Picasso was famous for

his cubism, a style of painting where the subject is broken up and repainted in abstract form."

"Chyah," said Tommy. "Total abstraction. I wouldn't even know where to talk to her."

"If I'm not mistaken," said Beck, "Pablo Picasso painted this particular watercolor way back in 1923. It was stolen from his art dealer by the Nazis during World War II."

Storm's photographic memory clicked in. "The Nazis 'liberated' this painting from a French art dealer named Paul Rosenberg because Mr. Rosenberg was Jewish."

"It was part of their organized looting of art objects," Storm continued. "The Nazis stole hundreds of thousands of art treasures, mostly from Jewish people, then stored them in salt mines and caves to protect their booty from Allied bombing raids. A lot was recovered after the war, but a lot is still missing."

"Like this one," said Beck, gesturing at the giant Picasso painting in the Chinese art gallery's display window.

"Hey," I said, "if we turn this stolen Picasso over to that high cultural minister, he'll become an international hero when he returns the painting to its rightful owner. Maybe if we give him *this*, he'll finally give us the Ming vase we need to rescue Mom!"

"Worth a shot," said Tommy.

But the instant he said it, two gallery employees in white coats stepped into the showroom window and took down the Picasso!

CHAPTER 8

W e barged into the gallery.

"May I be of assistance?" said a very polite young woman in a business suit. She was wearing soft white cotton gloves and a big smile.

"That Picasso," blurted Beck, breathless with rage. "The one in the window."

"Oh, I am so terribly sorry. It is spoken for. A buyer has already claimed it."

"It's stolen art," said Storm, who's never been one for sugarcoating anything. "The Nazis looted it from its rightful owner during World War II."

"And," said Tommy, "in case you forgot, the Nazis were the bad guys. You ever see *Raiders of the Lost Ark?*"

"I'm sorry, but the Picasso painting, *Cubic Woman Selling Seashells by the Seashore*, has—"

"That's not its name," said Beck.

The woman smiled some more. "I am afraid you are mistaken, Miss—?"

"We're the Kidds," I said. "Maybe you saw our parade this morning?"

She bowed. "I am honored to make your acquaintance, Heroes of the People."

"Likewise," said Tommy, wiggling his eyebrows.

"However, as I said, the painting you are interested in was just sold to an anonymous buyer. For seventy million dollars."

"That Picasso needs to be returned to the heirs of its rightful owners!" Beck said to the gallery staffer. "It's stolen merchandise."

That's when four very burly, very muscular security guards—all of them wearing snug black suits and sunglasses and sporting soul patches—came marching over to scowl at us.

"Leave," grunted the head scowler, who didn't sound or look Chinese. In fact, he seemed to have a German accent. "Now."

"No," said Beck. "Not until you—"

She didn't get to finish that thought.

We were unceremoniously hoisted off the floor and hauled out of the art gallery to be tossed into the gutter, where we joined the soggy confetti and popped balloons from our recent parade.

Guess that's how it goes sometimes.

One minute you're a hero, the next you're being thrown out with the trash.

CHAPTER 9

On our walk back to the hotel, we noticed something suspicious. A street vendor was passing out paper menus for a nearby restaurant, but he looked *really* nervous.

Wearing a bright red apron, the little man was bald up top but had long, scraggly hair hanging off both sides of his dome. His wispy mustache was long and scraggly, too. His barely open eyes were darting back and forth like he was afraid the police might arrest him at any second. He was all kinds of jittery and jumpy.

"Please take one," he said, thrusting a stack of menus at us. "Crystal Jade Palace. The specials are very special today."

"Is this Chinese food?" asked Tommy, studying a menu.

"Um, hello?" said Beck. "This is China, Tommy. All the food is Chinese food!"

"Even at McDonald's?"

"Yep," said Beck. "Over here, Mickey D's serves bubble tea."

"The Happy Family is very good," said the spooked paper-pusher, tapping a dirty fingernail on the menu.

"What's a happy family?" asked Tommy.

"Us," I said.

"Speak for yourself," said Beck.

"What? You're not happy?"

"Uh, no, Bick. That art gallery is peddling pilfered art. We need to stop them."

"Actually," said Storm, "the Happy Family is a popular Chinese stir-fry dish, combining meats with colorful vegetables, such as broccoli, water chestnuts, baby corn, and—"

"Huh," said Tommy, cutting off Storm's recitation. "On the back, there's a special Kidds' menu."

"So?" said Beck. "A lot of restaurants have kids' menus."

"Not spelled like this. It looks like our name. *K-I-D-D*."

SPECIAL KIDDS' MENU 特別 菜單

TAKEOUT & DELIVERY

1. STEAMED EEL (ON RICE)
2. SWEET 'N' SEWER BEEF ← EW! ☹
3. SQUISHY FRIED SQUID
4. KUNG POW CHICKEN

"So," I said. "It's just a coincidence. Right?"

I turned to face the wizardly looking paper-pusher.

But he was gone.

"Okay," I said. "Maybe it's a clue!"

"No way," said Beck. "It's a misprint."

"No, it's not."

And right there, not far from Tiananmen Square and the Forbidden City, in the heart of Beijing, China, Beck and I launched into Twin Tirade No. 484.

CHAPTER 10

These angry outbursts are something Beck and I just do.

Constantly.

I guess it's because we're twins and so tightly wired together. Every now and then we, basically, explode.

Mom is the one who came up with the snappy title Twin Tirades for our manic meltdowns because: (a) we're twins and (b) a tirade is a harangue or diatribe (yes, Mom, our homeschool ELA instructor, was always trying to boost our

vocabulary skills) that's supposed to be long and acrimonious.

If I remember correctly, *acrimonious* means *nasty.*

But our Twin Tirades are never very long and not necessarily nasty. They're more like biting into a superspicy chicken wing dipped in sinus-scorching Chinese mustard. Your face turns all red, steam shoots out your ears, and you shout, "hot-hot-hot!" a lot.

Ten seconds later you're done and hungry for another wing.

"It is not a clue, Bickford! It's a typo!"

By the way, whenever Beck calls me by my full name, I know she's ready to tirade.

We ranted for a full ninety seconds.

But then my stomach started grumbling.

"You hungry?" I said.

"Yeah," said Beck.

"So let's go check out that Kidds' menu."

"Good idea."

And just like that, Twin Tirade No. 484 was officially over.

The Crystal Jade Palace was on the other side of the street, right next to our hotel. I was hoping today's special was something besides stir-fried pork and veggies.

I was hoping for a message from Dad!

CHAPTER 11

"Mmm," said Tommy, sniffing the heavily scented air of the Crystal Jade Palace restaurant. "It smells familiar."

"What?" said Beck with a laugh.

I was right there with her. "It *smells* familiar?"

"Actually," said Storm, "our sense of smell can trigger powerful and vivid memories."

"Chyah," said Tommy. "I remember coming here, back when I was a little kid and Storm was, like, two. See that lobster tank? I named the big one Binky. This was Mom and Dad's favorite restaurant in all of China."

"Dad really liked a waiter here," said Tommy. "Guy named Liu Wei."

"*Now* you remember all this?" said Beck.

"Sorry," said Tommy. "I'd forgotten all about this place until I smelled that stir-fried fish sizzling in hoisin sauce. Oh, by the way—stay away from the pig brains dunked in boiling oil. Even Dad thought that dish was too bizarre to eat."

And so we had our first taste of authentic Chinese food. Trust me, it's nothing like the syrupy, gunky, sweet-and-sour stuff you find at the Chinese restaurants in American strip malls. We feasted on Beijing roasted duck, all sorts of dumplings, steamy noodles, spicy Sichuan hot pot, pork meatballs, mashed pea cake, and, for dessert, candied haws on a stick (the red fruit of the prickly hawthorn bush, covered with sugar crystals and speared on a bamboo skewer).

As we were passing around dishes, everybody sampling what everybody else ordered, a frail waiter hobbled up to our table.

GREETINGS, KIDDS!
NOT THAT I KNEW YOUR MOTHER AND FATHER OR ANYTHING SUSPICIOUS LIKE THAT. WOULD YOU LIKE TO ORDER SOME MORE FOOD? OR I CAN JUST KEEP PLAYING HANGMAN ON MY NOTEPAD.

His faded plastic name tag read Liu Wei.

It was our father's friend.

Tommy smiled at Liu Wei and gave us all a silent signal—one that said, *Nobody jump up and down and shout "Woo-hoo! It's Dad's old friend Liu Wei."*

We needed to play this cool.

Otherwise, Liu Wei could end up worse off than those deep-fried pig brains.

CHAPTER 12

"Um, hello, waiter-type person," said Tommy, who's never been very good at improvising dialogue. "What else might you recommend from this fine menu of food items?"

"Wise elders suggest that you move on to the bird's nest soup and squab."

"Wise elders?" said Beck, arching an eyebrow. "Any fatherly type people we might know?"

"Perhaps," said Liu Wei cryptically, which, I've learned, is how a lot of spy people say stuff. "This wise teacher is a steady hand to have at the helm whenever you fear your ship is *lost*."

Okay. I know spy talk when I hear it. Liu Wei was definitely talking about Dad, the captain of *The Lost*, who manned its helm up until that night he disappeared in the storm.

"I was right," I mumbled out loud. "Dad is so totally still alive!"

The others shot me a look. They were right, too. I wasn't being cool like I was supposed to.

"Sorry."

Tommy calmly ordered the food that Liu Wei had suggested: bird's nest soup and squab.

The "waiter" bowed and bustled away.

"Um," said Tommy, "anybody know what squab is?"

"Pigeon," said Storm, very matter-of-factly. "A pathetic winged creature. A flying rat. An urban seagull. An ugly—"

"We get it," said Beck. "You don't like pigeons."

"One pooped in my hair in Paris. I'll never forget its face. Or its satisfied smile as it flew away…"

Yep. That's the downside of having a photographic memory: There are some pictures you can't erase even though you wish you could.

We ate our bird's nest soup and squab.

Okay, we looked at it. None of us were too hungry for anything "birdy" after Storm's little monologue.

"You think there might be a Dairy Queen around here?" said Tommy.

"Wait," I said, staring at the soup sitting in a bowl made out of crispy twigs soaked in broth. "This bird's nest has to be a clue."

"The squab, too," added Beck, who, of course, was thinking the same kinds of thoughts I was thinking. It's a twin thing.

"Maybe Dad is trying to tell us what treasure to hunt for next!" I said.

"Seriously?" said Storm. "What, the lost Imperial Pigeon Eggs of Russian Tsar Alexander the Third? I don't remember seeing those on Dad's list."

"Dudes!" said Tommy. "I've got it. Maybe he already found the eggs. In a bird's nest."

"What?" said Beck.

"The Bird's Nest is what everybody called the Beijing National Stadium during the 2008 Olympic Games."

"So?" said Beck.

Tommy grinned. "So maybe Dad found those jewel-encrusted Russian pigeon eggs Storm was talking about and hid them at the stadium. Maybe he buried them in the end zone!"

"This is China, Tommy," said Beck. "They don't play American football."

"So?"

"So they don't have end zones."

"Okay. Maybe he stashed the jewel-encrusted pigeon eggs in the locker room!"

That's when (fortunately) Liu Wei came back to our table.

"Do not visit the Bird's Nest," he said very softly, his eyes flitting back and forth as he checked out the other diners.

"Where *should* we go?" I whispered.

Liu Wei smiled like a wise *shīfu*, which is Chinese for *respected teacher*.

"Let fortune be your guide," he said.

With that, he presented us with a tiny lacquer tray. Four cellophane-wrapped fortune cookies were sitting on it.

"Um, people in China don't really do the whole fortune cookie thing," said Storm. "They think finding little slips of crinkled paper stuck inside food is gross. Means the chef was sort of sloppy."

"This is a special treat for our distinguished American visitors," said Liu Wei with a grin. "*Very* special."

CHAPTER 13

"You guys?" said Tommy as the rest of us grabbed our fortune cookies off the tray. "We need to leave."

I wanted to tear the wrapper off my fortune cookie. I was thinking Dad had stuffed a top secret message inside it. "Wait, Tommy. We should—"

"Now," he said firmly.

All those years manning the spyglass up on the poop deck of *The Lost* had given Tommy albatross eyes. He can spot trouble coming from ten nautical miles away.

I looked around and noticed several diners at nearby tables were staring at us. One was working his phone, trying to cover up his frantic conversation with his hand.

Liu Wei bowed quickly and dashed to the kitchen.

The four of us scooped up our shrink-wrapped cookies and stuffed them into our pockets.

Tommy dropped a stack of yuan bills on the table, more than enough to cover the cost of our meal.

Dozens of eyes following us, we strolled casually toward the front of the restaurant. Tommy started whistling. As he went to push the door, someone out on the sidewalk yanked it open—tearing the handle out of Tommy's hand.

The four soul-patched goons from the art gallery.

"Thieves!" shouted Beck.

"Dàozéi!" cried Storm. *"Dàozéi!"*

(I figure that's how you hollered "thieves!" in Chinese.)

As the goons closed in, Tommy yelled, "Run!"

CHAPTER 14

"Kitchen!" barked Tommy.

The four of us spun around and tore through the tight maze of tables. Fortunately, our pursuers were big and beefy and had trouble negotiating the same narrow lanes. They bumped into tables, tipped over steaming trays of squid, and took out the lobster tank.

Fortune cookies secure in our pockets, we raced through a pair of swinging doors to the kitchen. The air was thick with steam coming up from all the boiling dumplings. Chefs were stirring flaming woks.

"Back door!" shouted Tommy.

We dove through it.

And found ourselves in an alley.

"We're behind our hotel," said Storm.

We heard the kitchen doors swing open. I whirled around.

The four warriors of the art gallery were hot on our trail. One had a lobster clamped to his left shoe.

"Up to our room!" shouted Tommy.

We ran up the alley to the street, rounded the bend, and headed for the hotel entrance. Spinning through the revolving doors, we flew across the lobby.

A bell dinged.

"Elevators!" shouted Tommy, who really is a good captain, even without a ship.

The four of us hopped in, just as the doors slid shut—right in the four gallery goons' faces.

Getting off on the seventeenth floor, we hurried down the corridor to our room. Two very beefy men in black suits were standing in the hallway, their arms crossed genie-style over their chests.

They hadn't been there when we left the hotel in the morning.

Had our pursuers beaten us up to the seventeenth floor?

No. These guys didn't have soul patches. They also looked Chinese.

"Are you the Kidds?" asked one of the gigantic men, lowering his sunglasses.

"That's right," said Tommy, while the rest of us caught our breath.

"Welcome, honored guests. We have been assigned to be of service during the remainder of your heroic stay in our beloved homeland."

The elevator bell dinged again.

"Swell," said Storm, jabbing a thumb over her shoulder. "Start with tossing out the trash."

CHAPTER 15

Tommy swiped his hotel card key.

The lock clicked open.

The four of us practically leaped into our room and slammed the door shut.

Out in the hallway, we could hear our goons telling the art gallery's goons to go away. I think our goons had better weapons. After grumbling something like, "Tell zee *Kinder* to stay away from our boss's loot or there will be *ernsthafte Konsequenzen*," the stump-necked art gallery musclemen stomped away.

We were safe.

"So what's an *ernsthafte Konsequenzen*?" asked Tommy.

"Some kind of pastry?" I suggested.

"No," said Storm. "'Serious consequences.'"

Tommy laughed. "Aren't they always?"

It was time to open our fortune cookies, which were now just crumbs inside their wrappers.

We sat down in the hotel suite's posh living room (the People's Republic of China was treating us like royalty, even though they don't really have royalty in Communist countries) and tore them open.

Beck and I got the exact same fortune (guess it's another twin thing).

"It's not very poetic," said Beck.

"What's it say?" asked Tommy.

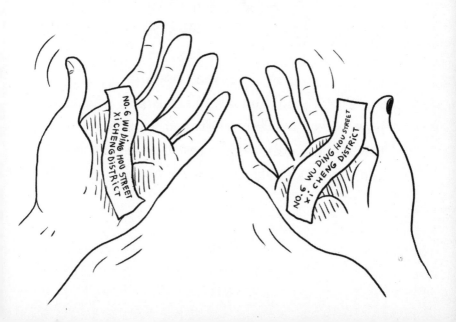

"It's an address!" blurted Tommy.

"Well, duh," said Beck.

I typed the street and number into my iPad. "Huh. It's the Beijing branch of an American bank."

"Storm?" said Tommy. "What does yours say?"

"It's totally random." She showed us.

"It says '*qībǎiyīshíliù*,'" said Storm.

"What's it mean?" I asked.

"Seven-sixteen."

"Cool," said Tommy, pulling out what had been tucked inside his fortune cookie. It wasn't a tiny slip of paper with words of wisdom, a street address, or a random number.

It was a small key.

"And look what's engraved on the head," he said.

"Well, what do you know," said Beck. "Dad has a safe-deposit box in China, too."

"That means he's here!"

"Um, not necessarily," said Storm. "He could've given those cookies to Liu Wei years ago."

"No way," I said. "They'd be all stale and moldy."

Storm shook her head. "Not sealed in airtight wrappers."

"But what about the rain slicker?" I insisted. "Dad's secret message: me in China."

Yes, that was my big piece of evidence proving Dad was still alive. He had scratched out the *A-D* on the MADE IN CHINA label inside the rain slicker he'd been wearing the night of the big tropical storm, the last time any of us saw him.

What could be important enough for our father to abandon his four children, not to mention his beloved ship, *The Lost*? How about his spy boss, Uncle Timothy, being up to some kind of no-good, dirty double-dealing with some shady Chinese characters?

"Dad came here because he knew Uncle Timothy was up to something seriously slimy," I said. "Dad *had* to abandon ship to stop Uncle T. from doing whatever he was about to do."

"I'm with Bick," said Beck, which kind of surprised me.

"Really?"

"Yep. You've been saying 'Dad's still alive' so long you've convinced me. Plus, have you noticed how much Chinese butt Uncle Timothy has been kissing on a regular basis? So, come on, you guys, let's quit discussing this and go find Dad!"

"Yeah," I added. "This key is the first step on our next treasure hunt!"

There was a sharp knock on the door.

"You have company," grunted one of our newly installed security guards from out in the hall.

"Who is it?" asked Tommy.

A familiar voice said, "Your uncle Timothy. Open this door, Thomas. Let me in."

CHAPTER 16

I spent the next several seconds wondering how much of my anti-Uncle-Timothy tirade Uncle Timothy had heard out in the hall.

Storm, Beck, and I quickly jammed our "fortunes" deep into our pockets. Tommy hid his safe-deposit box key, then unhooked the security chain on the door. With a final glance to make certain we were all ready, he opened the door.

Uncle Timothy, wearing the mirrored shades he wears everywhere, indoors and out, strode into the room, followed by his own troop of security guards.

"Hey," said Tommy. "Uncle T. We were just talking about you."

"Is that so?" Uncle Timothy said to Tommy. "And what, exactly, were you saying?"

"How those sunglasses are probably glued to your ears," said Beck.

"Or stapled to your nose," I added. "You never take them off."

"Our friends want us to sanitize our trail," Uncle Timothy said to nobody in particular. "You kids ready to roll? The high cultural minister wants to see you again. He has a proposition for you to consider."

"Is he ready to make a deal for Mom's Ming vase?" said Beck.

"I think so."

"What does he want in return?"

"Your treasure-hunting skills."

CHAPTER 17

We were whisked off in a motorcade and ushered up a long hallway to the high cultural minister's office.

The second Uncle Timothy stepped through the door, Beck motioned for me to hang back.

"We should tell the minister about that stolen Picasso we found," she whispered.

"We will," I whispered back. "Right after we get the vase. Family first."

Beck nodded. The two of us entered the office and stood with Storm and Tommy while Uncle Timothy, still wearing his shades, smiled a lot.

"I thank you, once again, for returning our priceless national treasures," the head honcho of Chinese culture said through his translator. "They will have an honored position in the new People's Museum of Art we are currently constructing. Soon my new museum will be filled with the finest artistic treasures in all the world!"

"Indeed, it will be," said Uncle T.

"We are honored we could help in some small,

insignificant way," I said, putting on my best official speech voice. "For you see, sir, we are treasure hunters, boldly going forth into the murky unknown, bringing back wondrous archaeological artifacts the world considered lost. And now the treasure we seek more than any other is the safe and immediate return of our parents. By giving us but one of the Ming vases, you—comrade, honorable top art official in the People's Republic of China—you, kind sir, will be speeding us along on our noblest quest of all."

Yep. I was laying it on pretty thick. I smiled the whole time the translator mashed my words into metallic-sounding Mandarin.

Then the minister uttered one sentence.

"The Ming vase is yours" was its translation.

I was all set to give that an arm pump and a "boo-yah," when the translator added the minister's "but."

"But, first, you must prove to me that you—ones so young—are, as your uncle Timothy insists, the finest treasure hunters in all the world."

Tommy got a cocky grin on his face. "Uncle T.'s

correct, *señor Gran Jefe*. We're the Kidds. We're good. *Real* good."

"This is wonderful to hear," the minister said through his translator. "Mr. Timothy has told me of your father's many treasure-hunting maps. How you four followed your wise elder's guidance to find your way to Zheng He's sunken treasure ship. Perhaps your father has another such treasure-hunting guide hidden here in China?"

Tommy didn't take the bait and reveal the key he found in his fortune cookie. "Huh," he said. "I guess it's a possibility."

"This is wonderful news," said the translator, after listening to the smiling minister's next batch of words. "If you want the vase to free your mother, you will, first, lead my archaeologists into a place none has traveled for over two thousand years. You will find a way for them to open our first emperor's tomb."

"The Secret Tomb of Qin Shi Huang," said Storm, who memorizes Wikipedia entries in her spare time. "The first emperor's burial chamber is filled with riches because Qin Shi Huang wanted

to be an emperor in the afterlife, too. He built a whole underground city complete with palaces, servants, temples, armies, brass chariots, and mountains of untold treasure. Legend has it that the ceiling of his burial chamber is studded with sparkling pearls to replicate the twinkling stars in the night sky."

"Whoa," said Tommy. "Sounds like the pharaohs and the pyramids."

"Exactly," said Uncle Timothy.

"But the Chinese already know where Qin Shi Huang's tomb is," said Storm. "Under a hill near the ancient city of Xi'an. Why do you need us or one of Dad's treasure maps?"

"To find a way for our learned scientists to enter the tomb safely," said the minister's translator. "Without becoming one of the dead buried there."

CHAPTER 18

Turns out, Chinese archaeologists have already unearthed some of the first emperor's hidden underground city.

"They've been excavating the site for decades," Uncle Timothy explained on the limousine ride back to our hotel. "Back in 1974, a farmer digging a well near Xi'an bent his shovel blade on a life-size terra-cotta clay soldier."

"Wait a second," said Tommy. "I've seen those clay warriors, all lined up in rows like gigantic chess pieces."

I nodded. "Tourists are always posing with those things."

"They're very popular with visiting dignitaries,"

NOBODY TIP ONE OVER. It'd BE LIKE DOMINOES.

said Storm. "So far, the Chinese have uncovered two thousand soldier, horse, and chariot statues."

"And they expect to find six thousand more as they keep digging their way into the vast maze of underground caverns surrounding Qin Shi Huang's crypt," said Uncle Timothy. "But nobody has ever been inside what has to be the most treasure-filled tomb in all of China—maybe the world."

"What's stopping them?" I asked.

"Rivers of poisonous mercury."

83

"Wha-hut?" said Tommy. "The silver gunk in thermometers?"

"That's right, Thomas. The ancient Chinese believed the liquid metal would bestow immortality. So Qin Shi Huang surrounded his final resting spot with a moat of mercury."

"But mercury is poisonous, even just breathing the fumes," said Storm.

"Exactly," said Uncle Timothy. "And that's the big problem: How do you enter Qin Shi Huang's tomb without ending up dead like him?"

"Good question," said Tommy.

"One your father may have answered. If he did, and you kids can find his map for entering the tomb, you'll be flying off to Cyprus with a Ming vase in no time."

"And if we can't?" said Tommy.

"Then, Thomas, I hope you liked that Kentucky Fried Pigeon you ate for lunch. You'll be seeing a lot more of it. The Chinese will not let you leave their country until you give them what I promised you would deliver."

"What?" screeched Beck. "You promised?"

The limousine pulled to a stop in front of our hotel. Uncle Timothy opened the door.

"This is where you get out, children. Go find your father's map. Get us into that tomb."

Then he basically kicked the four of us out of his car and had the driver speed away.

I was so tired of Uncle Timothy and his dirty tricks. Sending us into a tomb filled with lethal poison? Promising the Chinese we'd find Dad's secret excavation plan? Making me even think about KFC Original Recipe Pigeon?

I didn't know about my sibs, but I was definitely not planning on sending out any "Happy Uncle's Day" cards this year.

Then I saw something incredible across the street.

Maybe it was all that angry blood rushing to my head.

Maybe I was hallucinating.

Maybe there had been too much MSG in the Chinese food we'd been eating.

But, believe it or not, I saw Dad! Right across the street!

I AM, ONCE AGAIN, ONLY DRAWING THIS TO HUMOR BICK. HE'S SEEING THINGS.

CHAPTER 19

I swear it was him!

He was standing in front of the art gallery we'd been kicked out of. His baseball cap had a big letter *D* on it. *D* for *Dad*! And, get this: He was flapping his arms like a big bird!

"Dad?" I mumbled.

He tossed something up into the air. A fistful of bread crumbs, maybe. Because a flock of pigeons took flight, lifting off from the sidewalk in a flurry so thick it blocked my view. When the gray cloud of birds dispersed, Dad had disappeared.

I ran into the busy street. "Dad!"

Somehow, I made it across the street and was standing in the spot where I'd seen Dad.

There was no trace of him anywhere.

I heard horns honk and tires squeal.

Tommy, Beck, and Storm were racing across the street behind me.

"Are you okay, little brother?" said Tommy.

"It was Dad," I said. "He was standing right in front of that window flapping his arms."

Tommy put his hand on my shoulder. "Hey, Bick, for what it's worth, I believe you."

"Did you see Dad over here, too?"

"No. I don't believe that part. But, I think you and Beck are right. Dad is somewhere in China. Just not *here*. Or flapping his arms. Or doing anything 'birdish' or dorky. But, other than that, I'm behind you all the way. Dad is in China. Just like his rain slicker told you he was."

"And we've got to find him," said Storm.

"Wait," I said. "You believe me, too?"

Storm nodded.

"We all believe you," said Beck. "That's what families do. We believe in one another even when everybody else thinks we're nuts."

And then, right there on the bustling sidewalks of Beijing, we had an official Kidd family group hug.

"Okay," I said, after we'd all hugged it out, "now what? Do you guys think Dad really knew how to enter Qin Shi Huang's tomb without dying of mercury poisoning?"

"Definitely," said Storm.

I noticed that she had pulled out her fortune cookie fortune and was studying it again.

"Did anybody else get a string of Lucky Numbers on the back of their fortune?" she asked.

"Yeah," I said, looking at mine. "They do that all the time in Chinese restaurants."

"And sometimes," said Beck, "on the back, they also teach you Chinese conversational phrases."

"True," said Storm. "And today's phrase is: 'Dad put the information we seek inside his Beijing safe-deposit box.'"

CHAPTER 20

Tommy put a finger to his lips.

He didn't want Storm to say anything else until we were somewhere besides a crowded sidewalk.

We hurried back to our hotel and into the elevator.

"Let's check out the banquet halls," said Tommy, punching the button for the eighteenth floor. "One of them might be empty."

"Um, why can't we just go to our room?" I asked.

"Earth to Bick," said Beck. "Remember our brand-new security guards? Our room is under constant surveillance. It's probably bugged, too."

"And," said Storm, "with the minister forcing us to do this very important treasure hunt for him, you can bet they've beefed up our baby-sitting brigade."

We ducked into a huge and completely empty banquet room and grabbed a table underneath a landscape painting.

"Okay, Storm," said Tommy, "quick, before hotel security comes in to politely toss us out of here, what've you got?"

"Bick? Beck? Show me your fortune slips."

We both did.

"Flip them over," said Storm.

We did that, too.

"Just as I thought. The three of us got the same string of Lucky Numbers."

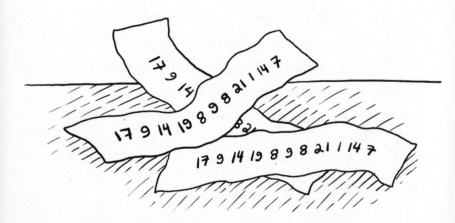

"What is it?" asked Tommy.

"Easiest code in the world," said Storm. "Alphabet numbers. The seventeenth letter of the alphabet is *Q*. The ninth is *I*. The fourteenth, *N*."

"Qin Shi Huang!" said Beck, so Storm didn't have to recite the whole thing out loud. "The emperor with the buried treasure!"

"Sorry, you guys," said Storm. "I should've cracked this sooner."

"Hey," said Tommy, who can be a pretty awesome big brother when he isn't too busy flirting or scrunching his hair. "You did great, Storm. And you did it exactly when we needed you to do it."

"True," I said. "Yesterday I would've thought that Qin Shi Huang was another kind of steamed dumpling."

"Or fried monkey butt," added Beck.

We were all smiling around the table when a woman dressed in a bright red business suit bustled into the banquet hall. She was followed by a couple of guys in military uniforms.

Uniforms that included pistols strapped into holsters.

"I am Jin Xiang," said the woman in red. "I will be your cultural attaché."

"You mean like a briefcase?" said Tommy.

The woman smiled. "You must be Thomas."

"Chyah," said Tommy, wiggling his eyebrows. "And there must be something wrong with my eyes, because I can't take them off you."

Our cultural attaché completely ignored Tommy's cheesy line. Guess it wasn't very cultured.

"Since you four are our honored guests fulfilling

a personal mission for the high cultural minister as well as the people of China, we will do everything in our power to show you our very distinctive Chinese hospitality."

"The soldiers, too?" asked Beck, somewhat snidely.

"The soldiers are here to protect you," said Jin Xiang.

"From what?" I asked.

"From whatever dangers might come your way."

I looked at the guys with the guns.

They looked pretty dangerous. And they'd already come our way.

"Please," said Jin Xiang, "follow me to your room. And, in the future, if you wish to sit in an empty banquet hall, kindly check with your military escorts first."

The lady spun around on her heel and led the way to the exit.

The soldiers flanked the four of us, then goose-stepped us out the door.

All of a sudden I had a funny feeling that our hotel room was now a prison cell.

CHAPTER 21

There were so many Chinese government functionaries, flunkies, and PR flacks crowded into our posh hotel room I think our official handlers had official handlers.

"We hope to make your stay as pleasant as possible," said Jin Xiang.

"You already have," said Tommy, wiggling his eyebrows again.

The cultural attaché pretended like, all of a sudden, she couldn't understand English. Or, at least, Tommy's version of it.

"In China," said another of our attendants,

"guests are always treated with great kindness and respect. You are also encouraged to do what you like!"

"Fantastic," said Beck. "I'd like to go for a walk. By myself."

"I am sorry, friend. That would not be safe. It is dark outside. Would you like something to eat?"

"No, thank you," said Storm.

"Speak for yourself, Storm," said Tommy. "I'm starving."

Storm held up her hand. "We really don't want anything."

"Um, Storm?" I said. "I'm kind of hungry, too."

Storm held her ground; something she does very well. "Thank you for your generous offer, friend, but we are not hungry."

"We insist," said a waiter pushing a room service cart loaded down with platters of steaming Chinese delicacies. He raised a shiny dome, and all sorts of delicious scents wafted through the air. Beef, pork, fish—all of it smothered with amazing sauces.

"Okay," said Storm. "We'll eat it."

Then she held her hand up to the side of her mouth and whispered, "In China, it is considered polite to refuse everything once or twice."

"But you said no *three* times," I told her.

"I know. I'm superpolite."

CHAPTER 22

O kay, official Chinese hospitality was awesome. Tasty, too.

Besides the great food, they presented us with all sorts of gifts. Our names painted on silk in delicate calligraphy. Boxes of Chinese tea. Paper lanterns shaped like goldfish. And those clocks where the cat waves its paw up and down.

On the other hand, a whole squad of soldiers was guarding us and making sure we couldn't so much as *sneeze* without it being monitored.

Beck flopped down on a sofa and, big mistake, propped her feet up on the coffee table.

Three soldiers immediately surrounded her.

"In our country, such behavior is frowned upon," said Jin Xiang with a soft smile.

"Look," I said, "do we really need armed guards to tell us to keep our feet off the furniture? Plus, we already gave you guys two priceless Ming vases. Do you think we're going to steal a couple of hotel towels or, maybe, a bathrobe?"

"The bathrobes *are* pretty awesome," said Tommy. "Plush."

"Okay," I said, "maybe we'll steal those."

Two dozen stern faces frowned at me.

"I'm kidding. We're the Kidds. We kid."

The frowns drooped deeper.

"Sheesh. You guys don't joke around much, do you? Soooo. What's on government-sponsored TV tonight? No sitcoms, I'm guessing."

THESE GUYS ARE TOUGHER THAN THE GUARDS AT BUCKINGHAM PALACE. THEY WILL NOT SMILE!

As you might've guessed, we Kidds really don't watch too much TV. We're usually too busy reading, studying, practicing martial arts, or diving for buried treasure.

But I knew it was time for a family meeting.

Someplace where our Chinese nannies couldn't hear what we were saying.

So I cranked up the volume on *Empresses in the Palace*, a Chinese soap opera about ancient intrigue and an emperor with too many girlfriends.

"I need to go to the bathroom," I said to Tommy, Beck, and Storm. "How about you guys?"

"Huh?" said Tommy.

But Beck caught on quickly. "Bick's right. I need to go to the bathroom, too."

"Good idea," said Storm. "Come on, Tommy. We're all going to the bathroom."

Tommy still looked confused. (Yep. That's why Mom and Dad nicknamed him "Tailspin" Tommy.)

I gestured toward the TV. "Let us know if we miss anything," I said to one of the soldiers.

He saluted.

"Pardon my question," said Jin Xiang. "Must you all go to the bathroom at the same time?"

"Yep," said Storm. "In *our* country, it is considered rude to go to the bathroom without the rest of your family."

I nodded. "We call it 'Happy Family Toilet Time.'"

CHAPTER 23

All of us grabbed our iPhones and headed into the bathroom.

Once we had all the water and appliances running, our Chinese handlers couldn't hear us. In fact, we could hardly hear one another.

Huddling together around the throne toilet (a rarity in China, by the way), we launched into a hushed and heated debate.

"We need to lose those people out there," I said as quietly as I could.

WE NEED TO MAKE AS MUCH NOISE AS POSSIBLE SO THEY CAN'T HEAR US IN THE OTHER ROOM.

Beck nodded. "We need to be at that bank first thing tomorrow."

"Well," whispered Tommy, "why don't we just tell the Chinese about the safe-deposit box?"

"No," I said. "*We* should go into the tomb first!"

"Bick's right," said Beck. "We should follow Dad's plan and bring out enough treasure to barter for the vase."

"If we give them the plan," I said, "they won't give us diddly. They'll just raise the bar and ask us to bring them something else."

Tommy nodded. "Like a sandwich or something."

"Riiiight. We just have to find a way to slip out of this hotel."

"And lose our handlers," added Beck.

"Yeah. That, too."

"I heard them talking earlier," reported Storm. "The guards were working out their shifts. First thing tomorrow, we'll only have two. They assumed we'd be sleeping in till eleven because we're 'lazy American teenagers.'"

They also assumed that nobody else in the room could speak or understand Mandarin.

"Way to go, Storm!" Beck and I said softly. Then we all gave her a patty-cake-quiet high five. "Excellent eavesdropping!"

"You know," said Tommy, who sometimes figures things out after everybody else already has, "Dad is helping us rescue Mom!"

"Exactly," I said. "He knew that leading us into the Secret Tomb of Qin Shi Huang would help us, finally, secure the Ming vase we need to bring Mom home."

Storm turned to Tommy. "So are we doing this thing?"

Tommy, the oldest, made the call. "Boo-yah."

"And we keep Uncle Timothy out of it," I added.

"Double boo-yah," said Tommy.

"All right," said Storm. "We better get back out there before—"

All of our iPhones vibrated simultaneously.

The four of us pulled them out of various pockets.

And none of us could believe our eyes.

There she was, smiling on the screen of all four phones...

CHAPTER 24

It was totally amazing.

Somehow, Mom, wherever she was, was able to text us a video message.

As the four of us gazed at her image in our palms, there wasn't a dry eye in the bathroom—and not just because of all the steam coming up from the bathtub, where the hot water was still gurgling loudly enough to camouflage our conversation.

I CAN'T TELL YOU HOW SUPERPROUD I AM OF YOU. ALL OF YOU ♥

"My captors have heard from their boss," said Mom. "He has told them that you four are very close to recovering the Ming vase they require as ransom."

"She's still alive," I heard Storm mumble. "She knows what we've been doing in China!"

When I glanced up, I saw Storm smiling.

When she saw me seeing her, she stopped.

Mom's video continued on the tiny screen. It was almost as if she were right there in the room with us. That she sensed we were holding an urgent family meeting and wanted to be there to guide us toward the right decision, something she always did on *The Lost*. Mom and Dad never told us exactly what to do. They just helped us figure out the correct answer ourselves.

"I want you four to keep up your most important treasure hunts, the ones that reunite family heirlooms with those who have lost so much more than gold or antiques. The Kidd children can be like the Monuments Men of World War II— the art experts that went into combat zones to save as much of the culture of Europe as they

could before the Nazis destroyed it all."

Mom looked off camera. I heard a man grunt at her.

"As always, they won't let me talk with you guys for as long as I want, which, by the way, would be forever!"

Another off-camera grunt. Angrier.

"Okay. I gotta go. Live good lives, children. Always be on the lookout for pathetic winged creatures."

Oh-kay. That was kind of random. Then again, Mom was always big on animal rights and sometimes sold her share of our salvaged treasures to help save dolphins from tuna nets and baby seals from worse.

Then, out of the blue, Mom started humming.

"What's up with that?" said Beck.

"Shhh!" said Storm. "I'm memorizing the tune."

"I don't blame you," said Tommy. "It's kind of catchy." And he started humming along with Mom.

Mom winked at us once and—*poof*! Our video screens broke into boxy squares of choppy pixels and dissolved to blackness.

She was gone.

CHAPTER 25

Note to self: A bathroom is not the best location for a Twin Tirade.

But that didn't stop Beck and me from launching into No. 488.

We were trying so hard to scream at each other *quietly*, both of our faces nearly turned purple.

"That was sooo superhelpful," said Beck sarcastically.

"Are you kidding?" I said. "It was awesome."

"No, it was weird. Why was she humming?"

"Because she's happy to be alive!"

"You mean she's happy to be anywhere besides stuck in a stinky bathroom with you."

"She's alive, Beck! She knows we're close to rescuing her."

"Well, why didn't she tell us what we should do?"

"Because she never does."

"Well, this time I wish she would."

"No, you don't."

"Yes, I do."

"Do not."

"Do too."

"Not!"

"Do!"

Then something weird happened. Instead of petering out and ending the way our Twin Tirades usually end, Beck started sobbing.

"Beck?" I said.

"You okay?" asked Tommy and Storm.

"Leave me alone, you guys," Beck blubbered. "All of you. I'm fine."

Then she started bawling her eyes out.

CHAPTER 26

Okay. This was freaking me out.

My twin sister is the strongest, toughest person I know. She never, *ever* cries.

Seeing her break down and weep uncontrollably crushed me to the core. It was like someone socked me in the gut and knocked all the wind out of my sails. Yeah, it's another one of those twin things. We share each other's worst feelings.

"Beck? It's going to be okay. I promise." I reached out and hugged her.

Tommy and Storm moved in, too.

None of us could stand to see Rebecca Kidd cry.

When Beck was all finished, Tommy handed her a towel so she could dry her eyes.

"You guys?" he said. "We need to find Mom and Dad. We need to put our whole family back together."

We all nodded.

Tommy kept going: "We need it more than all the pearls in the ceiling of that dead Chinese dude's tomb."

Storm grinned. "I thought you were going to say 'more than all the tea in China.'"

"Nah. I like coffee. And root beer. Root beer's good."

Fists started pounding on the bathroom door.

"Kidds?" It was Jin Xiang, our cultural attaché and chief babysitter. "Is everything as it should be in there?"

"Um, yeah," said Tommy. "We just need to, uh..."

"Find the toilet paper!" I shouted. "Oh. Wait. Here it is. Let me pass the roll around...it's another American custom...."

As we were getting ready to head back to the

living room to pretend to watch more TV, our four phones started vibrating again. Tommy had his out and up faster than anyone else.

"Mom?" mouthed Beck.

"Another video?" I whispered.

Tommy shook his head. "No. A text. From *Dad*!"

CHAPTER 27

T he screens of all four phones displayed the same message:

The last line was absolute proof that this text definitely came from Dad. Before he disappeared, he kept cracking the world's corniest joke: Q: "What's a Grecian urn?" A: "About thirty dollars a week."

But Dad wasn't finished. Another text message pushed the other ones up our screens:

"Pigeon races?" said Beck. "This can't be from Dad. He's too smart to write something that dumb."

"Actually," said Storm, "pigeon racing is quite popular in China. A shipping tycoon recently spent three hundred and twenty-eight thousand dollars on a single racing pigeon."

"No way. All that money for a flying poop dispenser?"

There was another sharp knock on the door.

"Kidds?"

Outside the bathroom, Jin Xiang was growing impatient.

"Just a second," I said. "We need to, uh, peel off an extra sheet of toilet paper for Beck."

She slugged me in the shoulder.

"It's for Bick," she shouted. "He's a toilet paper hog."

"Tomorrow morning," whispered Tommy, "we send the guards off to the pigeon races. Bick? Can you cook up a convincing story?"

I grinned.

Hey, making up lies is what I do best.

CHAPTER 28

I spent the night Googling "Chinese Pigeon Racing" so I'd have enough details to hatch a believable fib.

Turns out, a bunch of billionaires take their birds to Chinese "country clubs" and pay, like, a thousand dollars to buy their champion fliers a metal ankle band. The banded birds are then placed into pigeon coops and loaded up on a truck. When the truck reaches the starting line, the pigeons are let out of their cages. They take off in a huge flock and head home to their roosts, all the birds flying in different directions. Computers do the math and figure out which bird flew home the fastest.

Apparently, because there is no official finish line, it is very easy to cheat in Chinese pigeon racing.

Now, in some races, the winning pigeon can take home a million bucks. Not to mention what you can win by betting on the right one. That'll buy a bunch of birdseed.

It might also be enough to persuade our babysitters to desert their posts.

AND THEY'RE OFF! IT'S UH, ONE BIRD IN THE LEAD. AND ANOTHER ONE ON HIS WING. AND ABOUT FIVE BILLION OTHER BIRDS BEHIND THEM. THESE GUYS NEED TO WEAR JOCKEY UNIFORMS OR JOCKEY UNDERWEAR OR SOMETHING. I CAN'T TELL THEM APART.

The next morning, just as Storm had said, we had only two armed guards in our hotel suite. They both seemed extremely surprised to see the four of us up and out of bed so bright and early.

"Why are you awake?" the bigger guy asked.

"We want to go to the Pioneer Pigeon Club," I told him. "We have a sure thing in the third race. Tail Feather is the favorite."

The guard raised an eyebrow. "You wish to wager on this pigeon?"

"Nope," I said. "Against him. Rumor has it the fix is in."

"What rumor?" asked his buddy, who was suddenly very interested in everything I had to say.

"The guy who drives the pigeon truck says that when he reaches the starting line, he's going to give Tail Feather a heavier anklet band than all the other birds."

"Wait a second," said Beck, pretending to be shocked. "That's cheating."

"Yep," I said. "That's why certain individuals are paying the truck driver major yuan to do it."

"Why," said Tommy, trying his best to recite

the lines I asked him to memorize, "a heavier ankle bracelet. Will slow him down. As he flies home. To his roost."

Yep. Tommy memorizes stuff in chunks.

"It's a sure bet," I said, rubbing my hands together greedily. "We'll be rich! Rich, I say. Filthy, stinking rich!"

"Bick?" said Storm.

"What?"

"No way are the billionaire pigeon racers at the Pioneer Pigeon Club going to let *you* in on their race. You're too young. Plus, you're not Chinese."

I pounded my fist into my palm. "Darn it all. You're right, Storm. And it's such a sure thing. If only there was someone who's Chinese that we could send to the Pioneer Pigeon Club with our cash. We'd be sure to give them a generous cut for their trouble, of course..."

"I could place the wager for you," said one of the guards.

"So could I," said the other.

They looked at each other suspiciously. I don't

think either one trusted the other to share the wealth.

"We'll both go," they said together, in perfect English.

"Great," said Tommy, stretching into a pretty fake yawn. "Because, I don't know. About my siblings. But I need to go back to bed. This is way too early. For me to be up. I'm an American. And a teenager."

I handed each of the guards a bulging roll of Chinese currency.

They took off running.

ONCE AGAIN, KIDD CUNNING WINS!

We were, finally, alone.

When we were certain our handlers were out of the hotel, we all started laughing.

Something we'd probably do all the way to the bank.

The one with Dad's safe-deposit box in it.

CHAPTER 29

O f course, before we could go to the bank, we
had to get out of the hotel—not just our room.

Tommy stuck his head into the hallway.

"We're clear," he said.

The four of us hurried into the corridor and
headed for the elevator.

Which immediately dinged.

Someone was getting off on our floor. More
security guards?

"In here," said Tommy, jumping into a nook
with an ice maker and soft drink vending machine.

Beck and I pretended we needed ice. Storm
and Tommy pondered the beverage selections.

We heard a wobbly wheeled cart squeak up the hall.

Next came a knock on a door and a voice crying, "Housekeeping."

When no one answered, the housekeeper opened the door.

Tommy peered around the corner.

"She's in the room. Left her laundry cart in the hallway." He turned to the vending machine. "Quick, who's got change?"

I handed Tommy a pile of coins.

He bought a big bottle of something called Jianlibao Orange.

"Everybody—into the cart."

RUMPLED SHEETS, DIRTY ROBES, SOGGY BATH TOWELS. SMELLS JUST LIKE BICK.

"Tommy?" said Storm.

"Yeah?"

"You watch too many *Mission: Impossible* movies."

"Thanks!"

Tommy emptied the bottle of orange soda on a sheet and made sure the stain was totally visible before ducking underneath it to hide.

Storm hollered out a long string of Chinese words. Later, I found out they meant "Housekeeper? Take this terrible stain to the laundry immediately!"

Ten seconds after Storm shouted her command, the maid was back at the cart. She pushed us down the hall to the elevator. Once we were in the basement of the hotel—and right before we were dumped into an industrial-sized washing machine to be bleached and boiled—we tumbled out of the cart.

"Sorry," I said. "We, uh, got stuck in our bathrobes."

"They are very roomy," said Tommy. "And plush."

Storm translated for us. But it didn't really matter. The hotel workers were gawking at us as if we were crazy, which, I guess, we sort of are. Hey, you have to be a little crazy to be a treasure hunter.

Suddenly, our phones started vibrating again. Another text from Dad.

"'Are you at the bank?'" read Beck.

I picked it up from there. "'If not, hurry.'"

Dad didn't have to tell us twice.

"So long," I said to the laundry workers.

"*Zài jiàn*," said Storm.

And the four of us took off running.

CHAPTER 30

R acing up an alleyway and out to the street, we quickly realized that Beijing is huge and pretty impossible to navigate.

We didn't care. We were totally psyched.

Dad was alive. He knew we were in China. He might be at the bank, waiting for us.

Or was Uncle Timothy faking us out so we'd lead him to the safe-deposit box?

No. It had to be Dad. Uncle Timothy didn't know the Grecian urn joke.

Unless Dad told it to him, too.

I pushed all those thoughts out of my head. Focused on the positive stuff. Like, pretty soon, we'd all be reunited. Dad would show us how to enter Qin Shi Huang's tomb. Once we knew how to do that, the high cultural minister promised to give us the antique vase we needed to set Mom free.

By the way, have I mentioned how awesome our dad is? He's one of the most famous archaeologists in the whole world, but you know what he loves best about his job?

"I get to work from home and spend time with you guys."

Of course, our home back then was a sixty-three-foot-long sailing ship called *The Lost*. And his work was diving down to sunken ships or digging up buried treasure. But we all did it together. We were the Kidd *Family* Treasure Hunters.

"Who has the address to the bank?" barked Tommy as we ran past another jumble of signs that only Storm could read.

"Number 6 Wu Ding Hou Street, Xi Cheng District," said Beck and I, since we were the ones who got that info in our fortune cookies.

"Tap it into your iPhone," said Tommy. "We'll use the map app."

"Bad idea," said Storm. "In fact, we should turn off the location finders in all our iPhones—right now. Uncle Timothy is most likely using the GPS chips to track our every move."

Storm was probably correct. Bad guys had done that to us in the past. Especially with Tommy's phone. He's constantly chatting or texting or sending selfies to one of his many, many girlfriends, and that makes it totally easy for everybody in the world to track him.

We all pulled out our iPhones and switched off the location service.

"Guess we'll have to find our way to the bank the old-fashioned way," I said.

Beck made a stinky face. "What, ask directions? Buy a paper map? Wander around aimlessly?"

"Nope," I said, raising my arm and whistling loudly. "Taxi!"

A very suspicious-looking car screeched to a halt three inches from my toes.

"Taxi here!" cried the driver.

He kind of reminded me of a river rat. And not in a good way.

"This is probably an illegal cab," said Storm.

"An official taxi license is way too expensive," said the driver.

"That's okay," said Tommy. "We'll wait for a legal ride."

The driver looked like Tommy hurt his feelings. "Why do you insult me like this, you large-sized American man-child?"

"I just don't want to do anything, you know, against the rules."

"Like sneaking out of a hotel in a laundry cart?" mumbled Storm.

"And ditching our official handlers?" added Beck.

"And not telling Uncle Timothy what we're up to?" I tossed in. "Come on, Tommy. We're the Kidds. We live for action and adventure. We zig when everybody else zags. We're like the Wild Things in that book by Maurice Sendak."

"So let the wild rumpus begin," said Beck, sliding into the taxi. I slid in after her. Storm and Tommy climbed in, too.

Let's face it—we were, more or less, on the run from the Chinese authorities. What better way to escape than in an illegal car?

It was time for Mr. River Rat's Wild Ride.

CHAPTER 31

Even without a GPS, I knew where we were:
totally lost.

"We need to be at the bank!" shouted Beck.
"Number 6 Wu Ding Hou Street!"

"It's in the Xi Cheng District," I added.

"No problem," said Ratso, our driver. "This is
a shortcut."

He took another extremely sharp, tire-burning
turn. This time, we scattered half a dozen bikes,
made a bus swerve, and nearly knocked a traffic
cop off his pedestal in the middle of an intersection.

Storm, who sometimes gets carsick, looked greener than seaweed on moldy toast.

We kept bobbing and weaving our way through the crowded streets.

To make things worse, we all knew that Dad was somewhere right here in Beijing—maybe right outside our taxi. He could've been one of the people on the curb that our crazed driver splashed with gutter water.

"Don't worry," said Beck through gritted teeth. "Even though we're all probably going to die in this taxi before we ever see Dad or Mom again, I am not going to cry. I repeat: I am not going to cry!"

"Relax, kids," the driver said to the rearview mirror, totally watching us instead of the road and nearly rear-ending some kind of motor scooter hauling a cart loaded down with melons. "I am an excellent driver."

Storm had had enough.

"Stop this cab!" she screeched. "Now!"

NOT CRYING.
REACTION TO
CHINESE MUSTARD

The driver slammed on the brakes. We skidded to a stop in front of a very modern-looking building.

We all climbed out of the cab. Except seasick Storm. She sort of oozed out.

"Why'd you have to drive like such a maniac?" she demanded.

Our rat-faced driver gave her a knowing wink. "To throw off anybody who might be following you four—just as I promised your father I would. No charge—your father already paid."

And with that, he sped away.

What do you know?

Dad was still looking out for us.

CHAPTER 32

Tommy presented our safe-deposit box key to a bank officer, and we were escorted into a secure room behind bulletproof glass.

The walls were filled with rows and rows of small metal doors like you'd see in the mail room of a high-rise apartment building. Only, each of these doors had two keyholes. Tommy slid our key into one slot of box 716; the bank officer put his matching key into the other.

When they both gave their keys a quick turn, the small door sprang open and we were presented with a long metal tray.

Storm told the bank officer that we wanted a private viewing room, and he politely took us to one.

"Would you like some tea?" he asked as we sat down with our metal treasure chest.

"No, thanks," said Tommy. "We're cool."

We waited until the bank officer closed the door and left us alone.

It was time to open Dad's Chinese safe-deposit box.

Tommy rubbed his hands together, then raised the lid on the long metal tray.

Inside, there was nothing but eight paper birds. The box was our very own coop of colorful, folded chickens, swans, and cranes. One of the birds was even gray like a pigeon.

"What?" said Beck. "Dad went through all this trouble so we could come downtown and check out his most recent arts and crafts project?"

"I think it's cool," said Tommy. "Origami is so hard to do. All that folding and junk. You can give yourself a paper cut."

"Actually," said Storm, "in China, the art of paper folding is called *zhézhǐ*."

"Whatever," said Beck. "Origami or *zhézhǐ*, this has been a colossal waste of time."

"Maybe not," I said. "Storm, if you watch how I unfold one of these birds, do you think you can remember how to put it back together?"

"Definitely."

"What are you thinking, little bro?" asked Tommy.

"Well, the birds are made out of paper. Maybe Dad wrote something on the other side."

Three of us immediately grabbed a bird.

"Whoa," said Storm, who would have to refold them all to their original shapes. "One at a time, please."

I went first.

Under Storm's watchful gaze, I opened up the swan.

There was nothing written on either side of the paper.

Beck did the pigeon. Tommy tackled the pterodactyl (well, that's what it looked like). They flipped over their crinkled sheets of colored paper.

Still nothing.

My brother and sisters started to get that dejected look on their faces again. To tell the truth, I wasn't feeling so positive anymore, either. Why had Dad led us on a wild-paper-goose chase?

And that's when I remembered my purple pen!

CHAPTER 33

The purple pen was the only halfway-decent gift Uncle Timothy ever gave me.

Usually, on birthdays, he just mailed Beck and me a card with a packet of chewing gum tucked inside. Something cinnamony. You could smell it through the envelope.

Then, last year, since I was "always scribbling away in my notebook," he surprised me with an official Secret Message Invisible Writer Spy Pen. I guess they have boxes of them in the CIA office supply closet.

Anyway, when I write with my spy pen, the ink goes on clear. You can see what you've written only when you shine the tiny ultraviolet light in the cap on the letters, which makes them magically appear. It's pretty awesome.

Dad had used the same kind of invisible ink. When we pieced together all eight sheets of paper like a jigsaw puzzle under my tiny purple light, a detailed diagram for a high-tech and extremely incredible drilling device was laid out on the table in front of us.

It was a crazy, Leonardo da Vinci–style drawing of a complex machine—something Dad labeled S.C.U.B.B.A. The SELF-CONTAINED UNDERGROUND BURROWING AND BREATHING APPARATUS.

It was like a minisub attached to a giant corkscrew-shaped drill bit for boring holes.

"Those are oxygen tanks," said Beck, tapping the drawing.

I nodded. "So you don't have to breathe in the poisonous mercury fumes when you reach the moat surrounding Qin Shi Huang's crypt."

"What's with those 'hot air' thruster jets underneath the chassis?" asked Tommy.

"Makes the whole craft hover a foot or two off the ground," said Storm. "That way, you don't crush any artifacts underneath your digging machine while you plow your way into the tomb."

"I can't believe all the sensor gear in the control cab," I said. "Infrared. Sonar. With this machine, you could read what was buried in a wall before you tunneled through it."

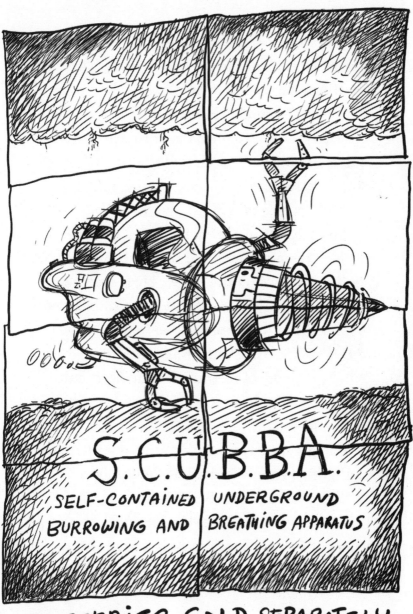

BATTERIES SOLD SEPARATELY

"And," said Beck, "you could use all the rubberized pincer arms to grab any priceless artifacts you dig up on your way in."

It was absolutely brilliant. Just like our dad.

"Okay," said Tommy, "it is totally awesome. But, could anybody actually build such a complicated contraption?"

"I think so," said Storm.

She picked up the eight pieces of paper and refolded them all into their original shapes. Then she started piecing the *zhézhǐ* birds together, the way you would if you were building a LEGO model.

When she was finished, we had a 3-D replica of Dad's S.C.U.B.B.A. drilling machine.

"We should take this to that high cultural minister," said Beck.

"Wait, you guys," I said.

For giggles, I'd been shining my ultraviolet penlight down inside the safe-deposit box.

"I see more words. Scribbled on the bottom."

Everybody peered into the long steel box to read what our father had written, maybe only hours ago.

CHAPTER 34

"So how do we get to the Forbidden City?" said Beck after we'd locked up the safe-deposit box and headed out to the street.

I shrugged. "Who knows? Maybe Dad will send another crazy illegal taxi to pick us up."

"Chill, you guys," said Tommy. "We have, like, six hours."

We had packed all the origami—I mean *zhézhǐ*—birds inside a plastic shopping bag the nice bank manager was kind enough to give us.

"You guys?" said Tommy. "I am so pumped. Bick was right all along. That scratched tag in Dad's rain slicker was definitely a clue. 'Me in China.' He is so totally here."

Yes, my chest was puffed up a little. I might've even strutted some. Until my twin sister shot me down cold.

"Even a broken clock is right twice a day," said Beck.

"What?" I snapped.

"Lighten up, Bick. It was a joke."

"Oh. So we're not going to have another Twin Tirade in front of all these nicely dressed business-people?"

"I hope not," said Tommy. "Because I'm starving."

"Me too," said Storm.

Tommy sniffed the air.

"Mmm," he said. "McDonald's."

Yes, our big brother has a very keen sense of smell. Especially when he's hungry.

"It's only ten o'clock," said Beck. "Dad can't meet us till four. I guess we have some time to kill."

"So let's kill it with a Big Mac," said Tommy.

"For breakfast?" said Storm.

"Totally!"

We followed Tommy's nose up the street and around the corner to the closest McDonald's, where, in addition to the famed apple pie, there was a pie stuffed with sweet taro, which are kind of like purple potatoes.

Tommy was able to order his Big Mac with a side of seaweed shaker fries plus a mint-flavored soda.

Beck and I went with dessert. She tried the green tea and red bean ice cream sundae. I had something grosser: green bean pie.

Mmmmm. PURPLE Potatoes. GReeN Bean Pie. SeaWeed Flakes on youR FRies, black and WHite HambURGER BUNS, Rice McRice.
I'M LOVIN' IT!

Storm ordered a windmill-shaped chicken-and-mushroom pie called The Pinwheel.

"In China," she said, "the pinwheel is supposed to bestow good luck."

"Cool," said Tommy. "Guess it's already working. Because today is definitely our lucky day. We're going to see Dad!"

CHAPTER 35

We wolfed down our Mickey D's and hustled back to the bustling street.

We were all psyched. Somewhere in the middle of this city of twenty million was one of the two people we wanted to see more than anything in the world. The man we'd been searching for across three continents and two oceans. The captain whose hat we had tossed into the Caribbean when we gave him a funeral at sea.

Our dad.

Guess we owed him a new hat.

Storm stepped to the curb to hail a cab, and before she even raised her arm, a rattletrap van shuddered to a stop.

Beck and I shared a twin grin because we were both thinking the exact same thing: Dad was watching our every move and had sent us another ride.

"Are you touris*tssss*?" hissed the driver, who was superskinny and had one of those bulgy Adam's apples like he'd just swallowed a hard-boiled egg. He also flicked his tongue across his dry lips a lot.

Beck stepped forward. "Yes," she said loudly, "we are *tourists*."

She said *tourists* like it was secret code for *spies*.

"We'd like to go to the Forbidden City."

We slid open the side door and climbed into the van.

"So," said Storm, buckling up her seat belt and pulling it snug, "are you a legal van?"

"No," said the driver. "I am an entrepreneur."

With that, we blasted off. It was time for us Wild Things to go on another wild ride in another unlicensed vehicle. Actually, this ride was even wilder than the one in the illegal cab. In a van, there's very little padding, so you feel every bump, rattle, and swerve.

"So," I shouted over the rumble and racket, "how long have you known our dad?"

The driver turned around and squinted at me. "Who?"

"Our father," said Beck. "Dr. Thomas Kidd."

Snake Face looked confused. "Who is Dr. Thomas Kidd?"

"Sweet," said Tommy. "Don't blow your cover. Pretend like you weren't sent to pick us up. You're a pro, sir. A real pro. It's an honor working with you."

"You children are Americans?" asked the driver.

"Yes, sir," I said. "One hundred percent red, white, and blue."

The driver shook his head. "No wonder you're crazy."

Sooo...

Turns out the maniac van man hadn't been sent by Dad. He was just a random lunatic without a license.

"A ride to the Forbidden City will cost you five hundred dollars!" Snake Face shrieked over the tortured squeals of his tires. "Five hundred

American dollars. Or Canadian. I take Canadian money, too."

It was, like, a fifteen-minute ride from the Beijing financial district to the Forbidden City. Even if we survived the ride, we were still being ripped off.

Storm was going green again—all the way to Level Kermit.

"Stop this van!" she shouted.

"What?" said the driver.

"*Tíngzhǐ zhè mìan bāo chē!*" Storm screamed in angry Mandarin.

The driver did as he was told. I think. I don't speak Mandarin.

Anyway, he slammed on the brakes.

"I memorized the Beijing street map," Storm said when we were safely parked at the curb. "And you, sir, are purposely taking us on a ridiculously serpentine route, hoping to justify your outrageous fare."

Now Snake Face smiled. Two of his teeth were extremely pointy.

"Fine," said Storm. "You'll get your money if

you take us to the Forbidden City. Now. No more twists, no more turns. And watch out for the potholes."

"No problem." The driver slid the transmission into drive. We rumbled forward, in a straight line, for, like, thirty seconds.

"Here you are. Forbidden City."

Storm yanked up the handle on the sliding door. "Pay him, Tommy."

Tommy peeled five crisp bills off his money roll.

"What?" said the driver. "No tip?"

"Sure," said Beck. "Here's a tip: Don't ever mess with my sister again."

CHAPTER 36

We were so close.

The Forbidden City.

3:50 PM.

Only ten more minutes and we'd be reunited with our dad.

The four of us stood together, smiling like crazy in the massive plaza, which was packed with hundreds of tourists, all of them snapping phone pics of what used to be the imperial palace for all the emperors of China—from the Ming Dynasty to the end of the Qing Dynasty.

(That last factoid courtesy of Storm, who, of course, had a billion of them.)

As interesting as Storm's tour-guide trivia was, none of us was really listening to her fun facts to know and tell. I don't think *Storm* was even listening to Storm.

We were going to see Dad!

It was 3:59. Any second now.

Any second.

He should be walking across the plaza.

In a minute.

Maybe he couldn't find a taxi or van. Not even an illegal one.

Maybe he got stuck in traffic.

Because, pretty soon, it was 4:05.

Then 4:10.

Still no Dad.

I wondered if he stopped by one of the souvenir stalls to pick us up a small gift like so many dads do when they go away on business trips.

Beck tried texting him, but she just got an error message that said "Not delivered."

We watched the tourists swarm into the palace museum.

We watched them swarm out.

We nibbled on candied lotus root.

We listened to Storm's endless tour-guide spiel.

"...It took a million workers fourteen years to build the palace. It is called the 'Forbidden' City because no one could enter or leave the palace without the emperor's permission...."

After about thirty minutes, our disappointment (and total boredom with Storm's blah-blah-blahing) was too much to bear. That's when Tommy proved, once again, why it's okay that he's our big brother.

"Hey—do you guys remember that time in Mexico when we were little. Mom and Dad found all those Spanish helmets?"

"And we wanted to play conquistador?" I said, remembering.

"I got to be Montezuma," said Storm.

"I was an angry Aztec," said Beck.

"And then that archaeologist came along," said Tommy, "the snooty lady from the big-deal college."

"And Dad stood up for us," said Storm.

We all smiled. It was a sweet story.

It was also pure Dad.

Of course, Dad made sure we never *broke* any antiques. But he always let us Kidds be kids.

Storm started humming that tune Mom had hummed in her video message.

"Dad hummed a very similar lullaby to me once," she said. "When I was a baby. In my crib. The notes were slightly different...."

Storm started humming.

Yep. Our big sister's photographic memory goes way, way back.

Especially if the memory is one she never, ever wants to forget.

CHAPTER 37

Pretty soon, it was five o'clock.

We'd been waiting for Dad for over an hour.

Just as Tommy said, "Well, maybe we should…,"
all four of our cell phones started buzzing and
binging.

It was another text message.

TOURISTS. ALWAYS TAKING SELFIES.

Apparently, he had a lot to say. The little cartoon balloons kept scrolling up our screens:

im ss.

I wsh I cud b there

ik hw mch dis must hurt u guys

it hrtz me 2

bt duty calls

Then, all of a sudden, he stopped using texting abbreviations, like he wanted to be sure we understood exactly what he was trying to tell us.

Push on with your plan. You have earned the urn.

Uncle T. will help seal the deal.

Keep going, Treasure Hunters.

Remember, the most important clues often seem small and insignificant.

A bird in the hand is often hiding the one in the bush.

Visit Bavaria.

The pretzels are lovely this time of year.

Safe travels. *Sicheres Reisen.*

The four of us kept staring at our phones, each of us hoping that Dad would start making sense.

But the texts stopped.

"It's code," said Storm. "Clues. Those last two words mean *safe travels* in German."

"So what's up with all the German stuff?" said Beck. "What's our next treasure? A dozen Bavarian cream doughnuts? And that bit about Uncle Timothy? Dad didn't send this. Uncle T. did."

"No," I said. "It's from Dad."

"It's a trick," hollered Beck.

And, yes, right there, in the middle of the Forbidden City, even with all its buildings and arches dedicated to peace and harmony, Beck and I exploded into Twin Tirade No. 491.

"Uncle Timothy is messing with our heads!" said Beck.

"Why would he bother?" I shot back. "Yours is already totally messed up."

"Of course it is. I'm related to you!

"And what about that bird-in-the-hand line?" screamed Beck.

"It fits with Dad's wing flapping in front of the art gallery."

"Which only *you* saw."

"Because I was the only one paying attention."

"You mean the only one spacing out and imagining things. And that's another thing. Why was Mom humming that stupid tune?"

"Because it's a lullaby. Dad hummed one just like it to Storm. Probably us, too."

"Of course he did," said Beck. "Don't you remember?"

"No. Do you?"

"Yeah. It was sweet. Got us to stop screaming."

"Really?"

"Worked every time."

"Huh."

Storm and Tommy hummed a few bars.

And, once again, it worked like a charm.

Beck and I stopped screaming.

176

CHAPTER 38

"We need to go see Uncle Timothy," said Tommy as we hiked away from the Forbidden City and into a busy shopping district.

"Uncle Timothy?" said Beck. "I don't trust him."

"But Dad said…"

"What if Beck is right?" I said. "What if Uncle T. is the one who sent us all those texts?"

Tommy shook his head. "I don't think so. That bit about the pretzels. When I was a kid, Mom and Dad were on some kind of treasure hunt in Germany. I remember loving the pretzels."

"What?"

"They were big and chewy and smelled like fresh baked bread. Sort of yeasty."

"You remember pretzels?"

"Hey, I may not have a photographic memory like Storm. But I think I might have a 'food-o-graphic' one, you know? Like when we walked into that Chinese restaurant. Or Louie Louie's Surf Shack down in the Cayman Islands. I never forget the scent of a good meal or delicious snack food item."

"You guys?" said Storm. "We're being watched again."

In front of us, two Chinese men were pretending to read the newspaper while peering over the top of the pages so they could read us.

A surveillance team.

I turned around. Okay, there was another team tailing us. No, two teams.

To our left? Surveillance team number four—a pair of those bulky bodybuilders with the tiny soul patches from the art gallery. It was really starting to feel like everybody in Beijing was watching our every move—and that's a lot of surveillance.

"Now what?" said Beck.

"Easy," said Tommy. "We go shopping."

Turns out, we had ended up in the unbelievably busy Wangfujing (try saying that three times fast) District—a stretch of cool shops that's insanely popular with tourists and locals. We pretended to casually stroll along and check out the street grub stalls.

"Anybody else want a meat kebab?" asked Storm. "Maybe some fruit on a stick? A bite of *baodu*?"

"What's that?" I asked.

"Quick-boiled tripe."

"And what's tripe?"

"The stomach lining of a cow or a sheep."

Storm. She really tells it like it is, even when you wish she wouldn't.

"You guys?" said Tommy. He gestured to his left and right, then his front and back. Yep. We were surrounded. The four surveillance teams were still tailing us and tightening their circle.

"So," said Beck, "this is like a pedestrian mall?"

"Correct," said Storm. "Cars aren't allowed on this stretch of the street. It's only for walkers."

"I think we're done walking for today," said Tommy. "Maybe we should run for it!"

And we did.

CHAPTER 39

*A*fter some serious running, we wound up at the Beijing Zoo, which, Storm informed us as we all huffed and puffed, used to be called the Garden of Ten Thousand Animals.

Beck tightened her grip on Dad's top secret *zhézhǐ* project.

"We can't let these birds fall into the wrong hands," she said.

"I am so sick of all this surveillance," said Tommy. "I mean, I like *girls* following me around all the time, but this is ridiculous."

Winded, we dashed past Monkey Hill and ducked into the Giant Panda Pavilion. We hopped the fence and hid in the woody stalks of bamboo while the pandas nibbled leaves.

"Tommy?" I said. "What're we going to do?"

"We can't stay in here forever," added Beck.

"True," said Storm. "The pandas may want to eat us when they finish their bamboo salads."

Tommy had a pained look on his face. This is how he looks when he's thinking. Like his brain hurts.

"Okay," he finally said. "Here's what I think. Beck?"

"Yeah?"

"You're the family negotiator. Can you make the swap—Dad's detailed S.C.U.B.B.A. plans for the Ming vase?"

"Definitely. But, we're going to need Uncle Timothy. The high cultural minister won't trade with me because I'm a kid."

I shook my head. "I don't trust Uncle Timothy."

"We have to risk it," said Tommy. "Dad wants us to move on."

"Germany," I mumbled.

"Germany," said Tommy. "Land of the most awesome, freshly baked, jumbo-sized pretzels in the world."

"Is that seriously all you remember?" said Storm.

Tommy shrugged. "I was little. Little kids like doughy, bready things."

"So we're going to Bavaria so you can eat pretzels?" said Beck.

"Nope," said Tommy. "We're going there because, I'm pretty sure, that's where Dad's headed next."

"You guys?" said Storm, remembering something. "Those goons from the art gallery, they had German accents."

"You think they're connected to why Dad wants us to visit Germany?" I asked.

"If they're not, it would be a very strange coincidence."

"Fine," I said. "Let's take our flock of folded paper birdies back to the hotel and ask Uncle T. to help us make the trade."

We said good-bye to the pandas, hiked out of

the zoo, and made our way back to the hotel.

And, of course, we were still being watched the whole time.

Surveillance teams can be really, really irritating that way.

CHAPTER 40

"Where were you, children?" asked Jin Xiang when we waltzed back into our hotel room. "We were quite concerned for your safety."

"So were we," said Beck. "Especially since you guys had so many scary-looking surveillance teams trailing us all over Beijing."

Yep. We Kidds can give as good as we take.

Uncle Timothy strode into the room. As usual, he had one hand to his earpiece and was jabbering gibberish.

Everybody in the room, including the Chinese, was kind of staring at him. Nobody understood a word he was saying. I sometimes wonder if Uncle Timothy even understands himself.

Uncle T. jabbed his fists into his hips and started barking at Tommy.

"Thomas? You're the oldest. I expected more from you."

Tommy smiled and nodded like a happy puppy. "Thanks, Uncle T. Appreciate that."

"That wasn't a compliment. I expect you to keep your siblings in line. Especially when you are the guests of a foreign country. You've completely embarrassed our entire family."

"Um, we're not really related," said Storm. "Remember?"

"Doesn't matter. You've upset your cultural attaché, Ms. Jin Xiang."

"Sorry about that," said Tommy, wiggling his eyebrows again. "Maybe there's something I can do to make it up to you. Do you like those seaweed fries at McDonald's? My treat."

"Thomas!" screamed Uncle Timothy. "This is serious business."

"Oh, I'm serious. I'll spring for a bubble tea, too."

"When you disappeared, Jin Xiang had no choice but to call the high cultural minister."

"Good," I said. "Call him again. He's the guy we need to see."

"Why?"

"We know how his archaeologists can safely enter Qin Shi Huang's tomb."

Jin Xiang and the guards, who had been whispering while Uncle Timothy ranted, suddenly got very quiet.

"How?" Uncle Timothy barked.

"It's a secret."

"One we're willing to sell," said Beck, "for exactly one Ming vase. And we want our urn 'to go.'"

Uncle Timothy looked upset. "Did you four children retrieve something from one of your father's secret safe-deposit boxes?"

"Why, Uncle Timothy," I said, pretending to be surprised. "Were you tracking us, too?"

"I am still your legal guardian, Bickford. I was concerned."

My turn to smile. No wonder Dad had sent Ratso to pick us up. The way he drove, nobody could tail that maniac.

"Uncle Timothy," bellowed Storm, "it's time for this surveillance to stop!"

Yep. She was in full thunder Storm mode.

"We're heroes. Remember? China gave us an official parade. We don't need babysitters."

"Now let's go see that high cultural minister," said Storm.

"It's late," said Jin Xiang. "He may already be in bed."

"So? We're bringing him something that's definitely worth waking up for!"

"And," I added, "tell him to grab an ultraviolet light or two."

"Huh?" said Uncle Timothy. "Why?"

"Because the cheap battery in that invisible ink spy pen you gave me for my birthday is nearly dead."

CHAPTER 41

It was around 1 AM when we had our meeting with the high cultural minister in his office.

As instructed, he brought along a bank of black lights on a rolling stand.

Storm flicked on the ultraviolet lights, laid out Dad's scheme, and explained how the whole S.C.U.B.B.A. contraption would work.

"Your father's plan is sheer genius," the minister said through his interpreter when Storm had finished and the regular lights were back on. "We thank you, Mr. Timothy Quinn, for leading us to this most marvelous solution and incredible invention."

Uncle Timothy rocked up on his heels and, once again, took all the credit for something he had absolutely nothing to do with.

"I told you, Mr. Minister," said Uncle Timothy, sounding pretty full of himself, "anything you want, I, or my people, can find for you. Keep working with me and soon you will have enough treasure to make your new museum the envy of the art world!"

Tommy tugged on Uncle Timothy's sleeve. "Um, just to be clear, when you say 'I' and 'me,' you still mean America, right?"

"Of course, Thomas. Now be quiet. I'm not done talking."

"Yes, you are," said Beck.

Storm scooped up the eight sheets of colorful paper and stuffed them back in the plastic bag.

I pulled out a bottle of water, unscrewed the cap.

It was time for Beck to close the sale.

"If Bick dumps his water bottle into this bag," she explained, "Dad's entire idea will vanish. Poof! Gone! Now, Bick doesn't want that to happen. And you guys don't want that to happen."

"No!" shouted the interpreter. "We do not."

"So let's make a deal."

And Beck went to work. When we were on *The Lost*, she was the one who always negotiated the best prices for supplies and repairs. She could even sell ice cubes to Eskimos. In about two minutes the high cultural minister was on the phone. In ten minutes we were presented with our Ming vase—all nicely packed with straw in a wooden crate with 脆弱 and FRAGILE stenciled all over the sides.

I grabbed the plastic bag with my bottle hand and, water sloshing, handed it over to the minister.

"Careful!" cried his interpreter. "We must keep the birds dry!"

"Don't worry," I told him. "I'm pretty sure that, for a project this important, Dad would've used the solvent-based ink. It's basically permanent."

"But you said water—"

"Did I? Huh."

The Chinese angrily left with their prize.

Tommy grabbed ours.

"Not so fast," said Uncle Timothy. "You don't know where to take that or who to give it to."

"And you do?"

Uncle Timothy smirked. "Of course I do, Thomas. I know everything and everybody."

CHAPTER 42

We headed outside with Uncle Timothy so we could talk in private.

We ended up under a streetlamp in an empty alley.

It was all very mysterious, and I wasn't crazy about doing anything that involved Uncle Timothy. None of us were. But it's what Dad had told us to do.

"If you four children truly wish to set your mother free, you need to do exactly as I say."

We all rolled our eyes. Uncle T. said that kind of junk *all the time.*

But if it would help rescue our mom, we needed to play along.

"Fine," said Beck. "As long as it doesn't involve wearing mirrored sunglasses and jibber-jabbering spy lingo into earpieces twenty-four/seven."

"I'm serious, Rebecca. Tomorrow, no matter what it takes, bring that urn thirty-one miles north of Beijing to the Ming Dynasty tombs near the Great Wall."

"Okay," said Tommy. "But, which wall are you talking about? Because, so far, I've seen some pretty excellent walls. One had all these neon signs and another—"

"Tommy?" said Storm.

"Yeah?"

"It's *the* Great Wall of China. There's only one. I know how to find it."

"Oh. Okay. Awesome."

"Stephanie?" said Uncle Timothy.

Storm's nose and left eyelid started twitching the way they always do when anybody calls her by her real name. "Yes?"

"You and your siblings need to meet me down in the tunnels of the tombs. I'll introduce you children to my contact—someone who is in constant touch with the men in Cyprus who are holding your mother."

"Can you really do this?" I asked. "Can you help us set Mom free?"

"Yes, Bickford."

Suddenly, a door creaked open. A very short woman stepped out of the shadows.

"It's true," said the woman. "Trust him."

I couldn't believe my eyes. In fact, all four of us looked like we had just seen a ghost.

It was Bela Kilgore.

A woman we had met in Egypt back when we were treasure hunting in Africa.

We all thought Bela Kilgore was dead because, the last time we saw her, she had just blasted out of a twenty-second-floor Cairo hotel window with a jet pack strapped to her back and landed head-first in the Nile River.

Usually when that happens, you die.

"You're alive?" said Beck.

"Never felt better," said Bela Kilgore.

"Wait a second," said Storm. "If I remember correctly—and I always do—Uncle Timothy was the one who sent that scoundrel Guy Dubonnet Merck to assassinate you in Cairo."

Bela Kilgore nodded eagerly. "That's right."

"Merck shot at you."

"With a silencer!" I added.

More happy nods from Bela. "Correct."

"Then," I said, "Merck basically made you jump out of a hotel window."

"Right again."

"Your jet pack fizzled."

"It was a new model. Still had a few bugs."

"And you crash-landed in the river."

"I can hold my breath underwater for three minutes. The CIA and several Navy Seals taught me how."

That's right. Bela Kilgore was a spy, too. In fact, she was our mother's "aunt" Bela, running her undercover CIA missions the way "Uncle" Timothy ran our father's covert operations.

"But," said Bela, "Guy Dubonnet Merck was an amateur compared to the vile fiend we have to deal with now."

"Who's that?" asked Tommy, sounding ready to take on the world.

"The man who holds the keys to freeing your mother *and* finding your father," said Uncle Timothy. "Mr. Dionysus Streckting."

CHAPTER 43

B right and early in the morning, we made our way to the section of the Great Wall of China snaking through the mountains just north of Beijing.

Tommy was toting the crated Ming vase. Storm was spouting facts.

First, about the Great Wall.

"It's the longest structure ever built by humans—five thousand five hundred miles. The Chinese invented the wheelbarrow. Probably so they could haul all the bricks to build this wall."

Then she filled us in on Dionysus Streckting.

"I did a ton of research on him last night," she said.

"And?" said Tommy.

"He makes Mom and Dad's other nemeses, Guy Dubonnet Merck and Nathan Collier, look like twin Santa Clauses."

"Nemeses are bad guys, right?" asked Tommy.

"Correct. And Streckting is pure, undiluted evil. His main business is illegal arms sales, but his 'hobby' is collecting expensive, no doubt stolen, art."

"Just like Athos Aramis," I said.

Aramis is the big-deal arms dealer and art thief behind Mom's kidnapping in Cyprus. We'd dealt with him earlier in our quest to free Mom and find Dad.

"You think Aramis worked for Streckting?" asked Beck.

"Probably," said Storm. "Dionysus Streckting is the big cheese, top dog, head honcho, and CEO of a major international art and ammo crime syndicate."

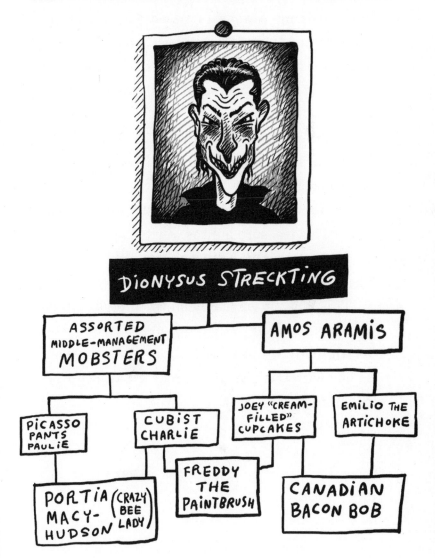

Storm wasn't done. "He's also stunningly creepy-looking: a weasel crossed with a badger. I hacked into Interpol's database, and Streckting is our most impressive and nastiest enemy ever. He should be considered armed, dangerous, and stinky."

"Stinky?" said Tommy.

Storm shrugged. "It's in his files. Apparently, he has odor issues."

"Too bad," said Beck. "We'll just have to hold our noses. This treasure hunt is way too important."

Beck was right. This was our ultimate quest! The Treasure Hunt for Mom and Dad.

This is what we had been training for all our lives.

And why we were willing to risk going one-on-one with the most dangerous villain we'd ever encountered.

(EW!)
HELLO, KIDDS!
ARGH DUDE!
CHOMP!
NEWEST ARCH-ENEMY
MOM AND DAD!
HAPPINESS!

CHAPTER 44

A s instructed, we made our way down from
the Great Wall and into the very narrow,
very deep, *very* spooky tunnels of the Thirteen
Tombs of the Ming Dynasty.

Yep. These were the catacombs where thirteen
dead emperors were buried.

Leave it to Uncle Timothy to choose a tomb as
a swell place to meet.

After trudging through a few burial chambers,
we came to the tomb room where Uncle Timothy
was waiting for us.

He wasn't alone.

Two of the Germanic goons from the art gallery were with him. So was a stunningly creepy-looking man with slicked-back hair. He sort of looked like a weasel crossed with a badger. I started fanning the air in front of my face.

That's right.

It was Dionysus Streckting. And the intelligence was correct. Even at fifty paces, he stank.

Like a clogged toilet. In a greasy gas station. On a hot day.

All four men were chuckling and chortling.

Tommy raised his hand. At his signal, we hugged the walls and hung back in the gloomy tunnel so we could hear what the bad guys found so amusing.

Apparently, the two guys with the soul patches, the thugs who had been chasing us around Beijing longer than anybody else, worked for Dionysus Streckting, too.

Beck gasped when she saw what they were holding. "It's the stolen Picasso! *Naked Woman on the Beach*. It's from that art gallery!"

"Well done, gentlemen," we heard Streckting say. "Well done, indeed."

"*Danke*, boss."

"Timothy?" said Streckting.

"Yes?" asked Uncle T.

"Cross it off the list."

"Consider it crossed off."

Beck had seen enough.

She marched out of the shadows and into the room. The four men spun around.

"You're going to give that back to its rightful owner. Right, Uncle Timothy?"

"Ah," said Streckting. "You're Rebecca, correct? The annoying, artistic child."

"So?"

Streckting grinned. "Nothing, dear. It's just that you look so much like your mother."

"Oh, really? How would you know?"

"Easy. For I have spent a good deal of time with your mother."

Laughing, he showed Beck a photograph.

Streckting and Mom. Holding a newspaper.

Dated yesterday.

CHAPTER 45

S treckting and Uncle Timothy seemed as chummy as a pair of poisonous vipers trapped in the same basket.

They sniggered when Streckting made that crack about our mom. The two German goons were giggling, too. But they had to. Henchmen always have to laugh at whatever their boss finds funny.

But Uncle Timothy?

You know all those bad things I've been thinking about him, like how Dad had to abandon us on *The Lost* so he could go on a supersecret mission to shut down whatever sort of shady dealings

Uncle Timothy had going on over in China?

I was pretty sure I was absolutely, positively correct.

Streckting drifted across the room toward us.

He smelled like dung. Cow dung. I think it was his cologne: Axe Cattle Spray.

He drooled a lot, too.

He also spit when he spoke. I guess because he wanted to pronounce all his words supercorrectly. Too bad he always spoke (and spat) right in our faces.

"So are you in charge of the gangsters who kidnapped Mom in Cyprus?" I asked. "We're pretty sure you are. We even have a chart. Did Aramis really work for you?"

Streckting just smiled. The guy was cold, snobby, and wicked smart.

"My dear boy, all you need to know is that I am the one person in the entire world who can guarantee your mother's safe release. But, it seems you puny, putrid, and problematic persons would like to know more about me?"

I wiped my face. There were a lot of spittle-spattering consonants in that last sentence.

"Very well. I have degrees from Harvard,

WHENEVER IT RAINS, IT IS BECAUSE I HAVE B.O.
THE POLICE ARE ALWAYS QUESTIONING ME BECAUSE I GIVE VERY INTERESTING ANSWERS.
I DOUBTED MYSELF ONCE JUST TO SEE HOW YOU MUST FEEL ALL THE TIME.

Oxford, MIT, the University of Tokyo, and several online schools of torture. What they say about me is true: I am the most interesting and physically repellent man in the world."

Streckting wasn't finished telling us about how wonderfully horrible he was. "I am also the world's greatest art connoisseur."

Beck stepped forward. "Then you know that Picasso painting was stolen by the Nazis during World War II."

"Yes. Poor thing spent so many years in a Hungarian salt mine. Now it will see the light of day once again. In a brand-new museum."

"But—"

"I believe, Rebecca," said Streckting, "we were talking about your mother?"

"Yeah," said Tommy. "Tell those kidnappers in Cyprus to let her go."

"Oh, I'll tell them, Thomas. And they will let her go. Just as soon as we do two little things."

"Name them."

"We must, of course, first send them their Ming vase...."

Aunt Bela leaped out of the shadows. She was wearing another jet pack on her back.

"I'm on it."

"Hand Aunt Bela the urn, Thomas," coached Uncle Timothy.

"But..."

"She will be our emissary," said Streckting. "Neoklis and Ibrahim are expecting her."

"Who are they?" I blurted.

"The Cypriot kidnappers," muttered Storm. "Duh, Bick."

"Your mother is my friend and colleague," said Bela. "I promise—I will not fail in my mission to see her released from captivity."

Somewhat reluctantly (because so many adults had lied to us ever since Mom and Dad disappeared), Tommy turned the urn over to Aunt Bela. She took off running up the tunnels. I hoped she didn't blast off when she reached the surface. We'd seen her go jet-packing before. Crash landings aren't a good idea when you're carrying a piece of priceless, irreplaceable pottery.

"Bela will make the trade for your mother the

BICK'S WORST NIGHTMARE.
(ACTUALLY, MINE TOO.)

instant I tell her to," said Uncle Timothy.

"And when will that be?" demanded Tommy.

Streckting smirked. "As soon as you four children, the Kidd Family Treasure Hunters, find something very, very important. For *me*."

CHAPTER 46

"What do you want?" fumed Beck.

"Something I had hoped your father would give me," said Streckting. "Unfortunately, he left China before we could...chat. Such a pity. He dropped his hat at the Forbidden City before my associates could arrange for us to meet."

"You mean he escaped before they could nab him," said Beck.

"Tomato, tomahto."

Streckting showed us a baseball cap with the letter *D* on it.

D for *Dad*.

It was the same hat I had seen Dad wearing when he was flapping his wings outside the art gallery.

"So that's why he didn't meet us at the Forbidden City," said Tommy. "He had to flee or your goons would've kidnapped him, too."

Storm took the hat from Streckting.

The way she was studying it, I could tell she was cross-referencing it against all the random images stored in her photographic memory.

"Let's not dwell on the past, children," said Streckting. "Let's just accept the fact that your father has, once again, abandoned you."

"No, he did not!" I shouted.

"Yes. He did. But I am not here as your family therapist. I need some vital information from your father's vast trove of treasure maps and rare

documents. Information we suspect he hid somewhere in Germany."

"Germany," mumbled Tommy (probably because
he was smelling pretzels again).

"Since your father won't give me what I want,
you children must go find it for me. And when
you do, I will contact Neoklis and Ibrahim in
Cyprus with final instructions to set your mother
free."

"And if we refuse to do your dirty work?" asked
Beck.

"Then, my dear little girl, I will call my Cypriot
friends with very different instructions concern-
ing your mother. *Painful* ones."

"That baseball cap," said Storm. "Dad was really
wearing it?"

"Yes," said Streckting. "I give you my word as
the most interesting and physically repellent man
in the world."

"Huh," said Storm. "Usually, Dad's a Miami
Marlins fan. This hat is for the German national
team."

"Ja," said one of Streckting's musclemen. "*D* for *Deutschland*. Go, Big D!"

The four of us exchanged a quick glance. We all figured the hat was another clue. Dad was telling us what to do and where to go.

"Fine," said Tommy. "We'll go to Germany and try to find whatever it is you're looking for."

"I'm going with you," said Uncle Timothy.

"Us too," said the two goons.

"*Wunderbar!*" said Streckting. "Now, then—off you go. See you in Berlin."

Uncle Timothy led the way out of the tombs. The four of us followed behind him. The two obviously armed guards brought up the rear.

As we climbed up a set of dark steps, Storm handed me the baseball cap.

"Check out the tag," she whispered.

I glanced inside the hatband.

I smiled.

Dad was sending us another message: ME IN GERMANY!

PART 2

THE QUEST FOR THE BIRD'S NEST

CHAPTER 47

$\mathcal{A}$ h, Germany!

After a ten-hour flight from Beijing (with Uncle Timothy totally hogging the armrest), we arrived in Berlin.

Yep. We traveled all the way from the Great Wall to the Berlin Wall.

Actually, it was the Berlin Wall *memorial* on Bernauer Strasse, a street in the German capital.

"This is the last chunk of the barricade still standing," explained Storm. "The rest of the wall— a fortified border of concrete, steel spikes, guard towers, and barbed wire—was torn down in 1989."

It was extremely cool to be in Berlin, where President Kennedy once declared, *"Ich bin ein Berliner"* (which, Storm assured us, meant "I am one with the people of Berlin" and not "I am a jelly doughnut," even though a *berliner is* a very popular jelly-filled pastry in Germany).

But how were we ever going to find whatever it was that the disgustingly stinky Dionysus Streckting wanted us to dig up for him before he'd set Mom free?

So far, the most physically repellent man in the world hadn't been very specific. He just kept saying,

"I need for you four to find what I suspect your famous father has already found!"

He also sprayed us with a salvo of saliva every time he said one of those *s* or *f* words.

We'd been at the Berlin Wall memorial only about fifteen minutes before Streckting and his crew of stump-necked flunkies strode across the street to greet us. The thugs we first met at the art gallery in China were still with him. So was a new short and stubby guy.

"Welcome to Berlin," said Streckting. "This Tyrolean troll is my trusted lieutenant, Franz Hans Keplernicht. He will be supervising you children from now on. I am far too busy master-minding evil plots to be a babysitter."

"What about Uncle Timothy?" asked Tommy.

"Timothy and I have nefarious schemes that require our undivided attention."

"Roger that," said Uncle T., who wasn't even pretending to be one of the good guys anymore.

"Besides," said Streckting, "Franz Hans enjoys working with children."

231

"*Ja,*" said Franz Hans, clicking his boot heels together. "Children *und* small dogs."

"What about Mom?" I snapped.

Streckting smirked. "Find what *I* want and I will give you what *you* want."

"Okay," said Tommy. "But, um, what exactly are we looking for?"

"The greatest treasure in all of Germany, maybe the world!"

"Could you be a little more vague?" said Storm sarcastically.

Streckting ignored her. "Timothy? Time to go. Franz Hans? Mind the children."

"Yes, sir!" shouted Franz Hans.

Streckting gave us one last piece of advice before departing: "Find me my treasure, Kidds. Or the next time you see your dear mother, it will be at her funeral!"

CHAPTER 48

The second Streckting and Uncle Timothy were gone, the four of us huddled together so our German nannies couldn't hear what we were saying.

"Okay, you guys," said Tommy. "What's the greatest treasure in Germany?"

"Maybe the Amber Room?" said Storm.

"Of course!" I said. "It was on Dad's list!"

The Amber Room was this huge palace hall made up of mirrors and amber panels covered with jewels and gold. They used to call it the Eighth Wonder of the World. A Prussian king gave it to Tsar Peter the Great. Prussia used to be a kingdom inside what is now Germany!

"Wait a second," said Beck. "The Amber Room was *built* in Germany but given to the tsar, who set it up in a Russian palace."

"True," said Storm. "But, during World War II, the Nazis looted that palace and packed up the Amber Room panels in railroad crates to be shipped...somewhere."

"Maybe home to Germany," I blurted.

"That's my hunch," said Storm. "Estimated present-day value? One hundred and forty-two million dollars."

"Were there, like, bird decorations on any of the panels?" asked Tommy.

"Huh?" said the rest of us.

"Dad's been dropping a lot of hints about birds," Tommy explained. "If he wanted us to find the Amber Room, why didn't he dress up like a mosquito when he waved at Bick in Beijing?"

"Huh?"

Yeah. We all said it again.

"You know—from that movie *Jurassic Park.*

Where the scientists find a mosquito that sucked dinosaur blood."

"Huh?" This time it was just me and Beck.

"The mosquito is trapped inside fossilized tree sap," explained Storm. "That's what amber is— ancient tree sap that's turned golden."

"It was an awesome movie," said Tommy. "I loved the T. rex!" He started imitating the screech and tiny arm moves of a berserk dinosaur.

That's when Franz Hans Keplernicht and his musclemen made their move.

CHAPTER 49

We were shoved into the back of a van with Franz Hans Keplernicht.

One of the other thugs locked the rear doors and thumped on the side of the vehicle, and we sped off.

"Where are you taking us?" Beck demanded.

Franz Hans grinned. "The Alps. Bavaria! Home of yodelers, funny pants, feathered hats, and oompah-pah music."

Tommy gritted his teeth. "Are you trying to torture us?"

"*Ja!* Exactly!"

We had a horrible sound track for our Alpine journey: tubas, clarinets, trombones, and accordions cranking out a polka waltz.

"Please," said Tommy, "I'm begging you. Find a new radio station!"

"*Nein!* Soon you will tell me everything I want to know!"

A few nightmarish hours later, the van came to an abrupt stop.

"Out!" ordered the thugs who yanked open the back doors.

We were parked on a rutted dirt road somewhere in the woods, surrounded by towering pine trees and cascading mountains.

"Looks like the Bavarian Forest," said Beck.

"I've been here before," said Tommy. He took in a deep breath. "Oh, yeah. I remember that clean, fresh scent."

"The Germans call the Bavarian Forest their 'air spa,'" said Storm.

"We drove up here with our neighbors the Pichelsteiners," said Tommy, sniffing the air again. "Good times."

Franz Hans came around the van. "I hope you children enjoyed the ride."

"We didn't," said Storm. "Or the music."

"*Ja?* Well, perhaps you would prefer something a little more classical?"

"Sure," said Tommy. "Beyoncé would be cool."

Franz Hans chuckled. "*Nein.* I was thinking…"

He took a big pause.

(If this were a movie, you'd be hearing the "Da-Da-Daaaaa!" music right about now.)

"Opera!"

CHAPTER 50

S eems our German hosts had set up a terrible torture chamber in the basement of their cuckoo clock chalet.

They tied our hands behind our backs and duct-taped us into stiff wooden chairs.

"Soon, Thomas," said Franz Hans, "you will tell me everything you remember about your childhood in Germany."

"Ha!" Tommy laughed. "Never."

Franz Hans sneered. "That is what they all say until I play my special music. Then they all start singing like canaries!"

The opera started up on a scratchy record.

"Noooooooo!" cried Tommy.

His agonized screams were soon drowned out by the music.

Oh, the music.

Hour after hour of twittering opera warblers shrieking at one another in German while tweeting high notes that could shatter Coke bottles. All I caught was a couple of names like Sieglinde and Siegmund. I think one was a guy, the other a girl. It's hard to tell when they're both screeching like demented monkeys.

"It took Wagner twenty-six years to write this thing," Storm hollered.

"Nooooo!" screamed Tommy. "I can't listen to this for twenty-six years!"

And suddenly the music stopped.

"Now we eat!" said Franz Hans. "Unless, of course, you are ready to talk, Tommy?"

"Ha," scoffed Tommy. "Bring on the grub. I'm starving."

"Fine. But I must warn you: It is German food!"

"Noooooo!"

CHAPTER 51

I think the food was worse than the music.
First came the *sauerbraten*, which, Storm

explained, was traditionally made with vinegar-soaked horse meat. Next up was *schwarzsauer*, a German stew made of goose giblets, blood, more vinegar, and peppercorns.

The all-you-can-choke-down buffet wouldn't end.

We were forced to feast on some kind of white sausages that resembled a biology project about goat intestines, followed by *braunschweiger*—a slimy, spreadable meat goop unlike anything you've ever seen inside a shrink-wrapped box of Lunchables.

"Dig in!" said Franz Hans as the armed thugs brought out more platters of greasy sausages, potato pancakes, *currywurst*, *hackepeter*, and *kartoffelpuffer*.

When we couldn't choke down another bite, they took our iPhones, checked out our playlists, and sang all our favorite songs at us.

Off key.

They even danced.

Oh, the horror.

Then they brought in a big, fluffy German shepherd named Munch and wouldn't let us pet him.

"Munch is working," said Franz Hans. "His job? Terrifying you!"

CHAPTER 52

With all that food still stuffed in our stomachs (and Munch nipping at our heels), the bad guys wrapped ropes around our ankles and hoisted us up to the ceiling.

"Bad idea," I burped. "I think I'm going to hurl."

(Great. Beck wants to show you me hanging by my heels. Again. I reminded her that you already saw that, way back at the beginning of the story, but she says she's going to add a few more gory details. Obviously, I'm not going to do that.)

While we were dangling, Dionysus Streckting

walked into the Bavarian basement. Uncle Timothy wasn't with him.

"That is enough, Franz Hans," said Streckting. "I think Tommy is ready to talk."

"Yes," said Tommy. "I'll tell you all about my childhood in Germany."

"Excellent. Lower the children."

The goon squad did as Streckting commanded, then tied us back into our chairs.

"Start talking," said Streckting.

"Okay," said Tommy. "After all that torture, I definitely remember some stuff from my childhood."

"Good. Tell me."

"I had a tricycle."

"What?" said Streckting.

"It had three wheels. And streamers on the handlebars. I clothespinned a baseball card on it so the spokes would make motorcycle noises. I also remember this girl I met in kindergarten: Ilsa. She had curly blond hair and liked to eat her own boogers."

"Silence!" screamed Streckting. "This is not what I need to know! You miserable children will tell me where your father, the great treasure hunter Professor Thomas Kidd, has hidden the information I so desperately seek or my minions shall shoot you."

Okay, the "shooting us" thing was new, but, otherwise, it was the same-old same-old. And he still didn't tell us what the heck he was looking for.

"Do as I say or none of you will ever see your mother or your father again!"

"Dude," said Tommy, "what exactly are you looking for?"

"Yeah," said Beck. "Just tell us what we're supposed to find."

Streckting turned to Tommy. "You are such a fascinating boy. So, so interesting."

Tommy grinned. "That's what all the ladies say."

"I happen to know—and this comes straight from your father, who told it to your uncle Timothy— that you, Tommy, are the brains of the Kidd family."

Tommy? The brains?

You know those mass quantities of greasy food stuffed into our stomachs?

We almost lost it all when we busted a gut laughing.

CHAPTER 53

Wild, borderline-insane laughter erupted from the three of us.

"Tommy?" Beck was having trouble breathing, she was laughing so hard. "The *brains* of the family?"

"Uh, hello?" I said. "Earth to Streckting. Mom and Dad called him 'Tailspin' Tommy for a reason."

"Indeed," said Storm. "Typically, Tommy goes into a nosedive when presented with a complex intellectual challenge."

"See?" I said. "Storm is the brains of this operation, not Tommy."

"I would, however, suggest that Tommy is the *heart* of our family," said Storm. "He is also, when necessary, the muscle."

"And his brain is the thickest muscle in his head," added Beck. "Even if he never exercises it."

More gales of laughter. We were doubled over in our chairs, stomping our feet on the floor, whooping wildly.

Well, not Tommy. He was making a sad, puppy-dog face.

"Ease up, you guys," Tommy said. "Mr. Streckting is correct. I am, you know, brilliant. If you guys don't believe me, just ask Dad."

"Um, we can't, Tommy," said Beck. "He isn't here."

"Oh. Right. Duh. Forgot about that."

Yes, our beloved big brother, Tommy, proved our point by sounding like his usual numbskull self.

It was so funny, it even cracked up Tommy. Now all four of us were laughing so hard we sounded like hysterical hyenas watching funny cat videos.

When we finally quit yukking it up, Streckting moved closer to Tommy.

"You, Thomas, are brilliant in one very important way: You know more about your family's previous activities in Germany than any of the others."

"That's true," said Tommy. "Storm was just a baby when we lived here. Bick and Beck weren't even born. I remember our neighbors. The Pichelsteiners. They had a daughter, a little older than me. Her name was Petra. Petra Pichelsteiner. I also remember the pretzels."

"Excellent, Thomas. Now try to remember something useful. I want the treasure your father and mother were hunting when you lived here in Germany." He whirled around and barked at his minions. "Untie them."

Franz Hans and the other goons did as they were told.

As Tommy rubbed the duct tape goo off his wrists, Streckting grabbed hold of his chair and leaned in.

"Where did you live in Germany, Thomas?"

"Uh..."

"Try to remember. Frankfurt? Cologne?"

"No, it was...Munich!"

"Good boy!" Streckting said, as if to a dog. Munch·looked a little jealous. "Go to Munich. Take the van. Find me my treasure." He tossed Tommy a set of keys. "And Kidds?"

"Yes?" we all said at the same time.

"I will be tracking your every move, so act like your mother's life depends on it. Because, guess what? It does."

CHAPTER 54

On the drive to Munich, we tried to help Tommy remember something about Munich besides pretzels.

We played car ride memory games.

We did German license plate bingo.

Nothing worked.

"All I really remember are the pretzels," said Tommy. "They were so delicious. A crisp crunch that gave way to delightfully chewy softness inside." He sounded like a radio commercial. It was worse than oompah music. "I could smell them baking all day long...."

"And then there was the glockenspiel," Tommy mumbled.

"The what?" said Beck.

"The glockenspiel. Since it was summer, it would chime at eleven in the morning, then noon, and then five."

"Go on," I urged. "What else do you remember about the glockenspiel?"

Suddenly it seemed as if Tommy was being flooded with memories of his childhood in Germany.

"Tons of tourists used to gather in the square to watch it 'cause it had these awesome figurines that would swirl around and act out a story in time to the bells. There was even a joust with knights on horseback...."

While Tommy kept remembering behind the wheel, Storm, riding shotgun, started tapping on her iPad.

"I had a bird's-eye view from our apartment overlooking the square," said Tommy. "I used to walk to the window and see all those people and the glockenspiel and the pretzel café...."

"Was it in the Marienplatz?" asked Storm.

"No. I remember there was a statue of Mary on a tall column. Dad said the place was called 'Mary's Square.'"

"That's what *Marienplatz* means," Storm explained. "That must be where Mom and Dad had their Munich apartment."

Tommy nodded. "We were on the second floor. Right above a bakery…"

Finally. We were getting somewhere. And it fit with those clues Dad had texted us when we were still in China:

Visit Bavaria.

The pretzels are lovely this time of year.

Storm tapped and swiped her fingers across the glass screen of her iPad.

"*Woerner's Confiserie und Café am Dom,*" she reported. "It's a bake shop in the Marienplatz."

"Yeah," said Tommy. "Woerner's. Man, Woerner's was wonderful."

"Not as wonderful as you," said Beck. "Way to go, Tommy."

We followed the road signs for Munich and weaved our way through the city streets. In no time, we were swimming with the swarm of tourists milling around in the middle of the Marienplatz.

Tommy led the way into the residential part of the building.

"I always felt safe when we lived here," said Tommy, and we climbed up a set of stairs.

"Why?" asked Beck.

"I dunno. I guess because Dad called it a safe house."

"Uh, Tommy?" I said. "That's spy lingo."

"Cool. What's it mean?"

"A *safe house*," said Storm, "is a secret location where spies can safely hide contacts and informants whose lives might be in danger."

"Huh. Maybe that's why Mom and Dad were always so worried about the Pichelsteiners and told them to keep their door locked at all times. Maybe the Pichelsteiners were Mom and Dad's secret German contacts and informants."

CHAPTER 55

S ince Tommy learned how to crack open treasure chests when he was, like, six years old,
he knew how to pick door locks, too.

He jimmied a long, skinny file from his Swiss
Army knife into the keyhole and—*click!*—we were
inside Mom and Dad's old apartment. The place
was empty. Deserted. It felt like no one had lived
in this safe house since Mom and Dad abandoned
it to go hunt other treasures on the high seas
more than a decade ago.

But what were they looking for here in Munich?
Did they find it? If so, could we find it again for
Dionysus Streckting?

Tommy flicked on the overhead lights.

"Mmm," he said, savoring the yeasty aroma wafting up through the floorboards. "Anybody else hungry for a quick pretzel break?"

"First things first, Tommy," said Beck.

"I could go for a pretzel," said Storm.

"You guys?" I pleaded.

"We'll do pretzels after we find whatever kind of clues might be here," said Beck.

"Deal," said Tommy and Storm.

We fanned out around the apartment, searching in cupboards, drawers, and closets.

While we were nosing around, I couldn't help but notice the unusual wallpaper decorating the living room. It was covered with—you guessed it—pigeons. Some were hovering over bushes. So, once again, I thought about Dad's texted clues:

A bird in the hand is often hiding the one in the bush.

Is that why Dad was flapping his arms at me in Beijing? Or why he gave us the idea about pigeon racing to distract our Chinese handlers? Was he really trying to tell us to fly here, to their pigeon-filled roost in Munich?

While I was checking out the wallpaper, Beck, Storm, and Tommy dug up a few other clues.

1.

A jelly jar filled with ticket stubs from a local movie theater called the City Kino.

2.

Stacks of empty, grease-speckled popcorn tubs.

3.

The German version of the board game Clue.

"Enough with the clues," said Beck, sounding frustrated. "Maybe we should go downstairs and grab that snack."

"I don't think so," I said, spotting something interesting. One of the wallpaper pigeons was facing the wrong way.

Guess what happened when I bopped it on its bumpy beak?

A small, secret door sprang open.

CHAPTER 56

The cabinet was the narrow kind you could store a fold-down ironing board in.

As it flopped into the room, I noticed a rolled-up canvas lashed to the ironing board with twine.

"Looks like a painting," said Beck, our family art expert. "Help me out, Bick."

Very carefully, very slowly, we unfurled the canvas.

It was amazing. An abstract portrait of a Jewish rabbi done in bright canary greens and yellows and blacks.

Beck was kind of hyperventilating.

"OMG," she gasped. "It's a Chagall. It's a masterpiece. This painting has to be worth a fortune."

Storm nodded. "And, it's degenerate art."

"I don't know," said Tommy. "Sure the colors are a little weird, but I wouldn't call it 'degenerate.'"

As the family wordsmith, I, of course, knew that *degenerate* means *immoral, corrupt, wicked,* or *decadent.* So I had to agree with Tommy. The painting was a little bizarre, but it certainly wasn't as degenerate as, say, a sleazeball like Dionysus Streckting.

"Degenerate art," explained Storm, "is what Adolf Hitler and the Nazis called almost all modern art. They couldn't understand it, so they hated it. Many German artists were branded as enemies of the state and a threat to German culture."

"So the Nazis forced them to stop painting this way," said Beck, choking up as she spoke.

Hey, my twin sis is an artist. I can't imagine

how horrible she'd feel if somebody took away her pens and sketchbooks and told her she couldn't draw the way she wanted to draw anymore.

"Hitler's storm troopers stole Picassos, Chagalls, and Matisses from their rightful owners," Beck continued. "Mostly Jewish families and art museums. The stolen paintings the Nazis couldn't auction off at a high price in countries like Switzerland they just burned—the same way they burned books."

"Some of the so-called degenerate art was never found," said Storm. "It was still missing after the war."

"Like the Picasso painting we saw in Beijing," added Beck. "And now this Chagall."

"Do you think that's what Streckting's after?" I asked. "The art stolen by the Nazis? Don't forget, it was his German goons, not the Chinese, who chased us out of the Beijing art gallery. And now Streckting sent us here to Munich. Maybe Mom and Dad were close to finding the spot where the Nazis hid all their looted art treasures."

"The painting was hidden here recently," Storm remarked as she inspected the cabinet.

"Chyah," said Tommy. "I bet Mom and Dad stashed it here while they tracked down the rest of the art."

Suddenly I heard wood splinter.

A boot heel punched a hole in the front door.

Beck and I rolled up the Chagall as quickly as we could.

But it wasn't quick enough.

CHAPTER 57

Dionysus Streckting stalked over to me and Beck and practically ripped the canvas tube right out of my hands.

He worked the painting open.

"Ah. Very nice. Very nice indeed."

Now he touched a Bluetooth device tucked into his ear. It looked very similar to the one Uncle Timothy was constantly yammering into.

"We have the Chagall, Timothy. Kindly advise the high cultural minister that his new museum's collection of masterpieces continues to grow by leaps and bounds."

Was that what this was all about?

Retrieving art stolen by the Nazis and selling it to the highest bidder, who, in this case, just happened to be the Chinese high cultural minister with a new museum to fill?

Streckting smirked at Tommy.

"Well done, Thomas. I knew you knew things you didn't know you knew."

"Huh?"

"Never mind. You found one painting. Now you must find the rest."

Streckting had a crazed look in his eye as he paced around the room with his hands clasped behind his back.

"Paintings, sculptures, religious artifacts. Cubism, modernism, Dadaism. Picasso, Matisse, Degas. Hitler, the failed artist, hated it all. He had special units that looted art all over Europe and hid the booty in caves and salt mines to protect it from Allied bombing raids. Hundreds, maybe thousands, of pieces are still missing. Can you even imagine all the treasure waiting to be found?

"You children call yourselves treasure hunters. Don't you long to discover history's greatest collection of missing art?"

"Sure," said Beck. "But only if we can return it all to its rightful owners."

"Ha! Don't be ridiculous. Why would we want to do that when we could sell it for an incredible fortune?"

I raised my hand.

"Yes?"

"Um, is Uncle Timothy working for you now instead of the CIA?"

"My dear, innocent little boy. Your uncle Timothy has been working for me for years."

"And Dad figured that out," said Storm.

"Yes. Your father is a very clever man. He even faked his own death in that nasty tropical storm in a feeble attempt to make me lower my guard. When I realized he was still alive and trying to sabotage our overtures to the Chinese high cultural minister, I immediately flew to Beijing so your father and I could chat about the artworks stolen by Hitler and the Nazis. When I could not capture—that is *find*—Dr. Kidd to politely ask him where this fantastic hoard might be hidden, I went with Plan B."

He gestured toward us.

Yep. We were Plan B.

"Find me my missing masterpieces, children. Enough to fill an entire museum. Make your father proud—and save your mother's life!"

CHAPTER 58

And so we basically spent the next few days under house arrest.

"Can I go downstairs to grab a pretzel?" asked Tommy on day three.

"Nein!" said Franz Hans, who was, once again, put in charge by Streckting. "You Kidd kids will go nowhere until you take us to the treasure trove."

Franz Hans Keplernicht and his armed heavies hovered around the edges of the apartment, waiting for us to come up with a plan for finding and salvaging the Nazi loot.

The problem was, we had very little to work with. No treasure map. No clues, except for the pigeon wallpaper, the ticket stubs, the popcorn tubs, and the German version of Clue, with a Colonel Oberst von Gatow who looked a lot spicier than the American Colonel Mustard.

No new text messages from Dad.

"Think, Tommy," I said. "Remember anything you can, no matter how small or insignificant, because Dad's last text told us that the most important clues often seem small and insignificant."

Tommy nodded and said, "Anybody else seriously famished?"

Down on the first floor, Woerner's bakery was going full steam, distracting Tommy with its drifting aroma of deliciousness.

"No pretzels for you!" shouted Franz Hans. "Not until you find the artwork!"

But, even though he racked his brain, Tommy's memory of what Dad and Mom did while they were in Munich didn't go much beyond the baked goods at Woerner's, the glockenspiel and tourists in the Marienplatz, the Pichelsteiners in the apartment next door, and Munich's Oktoberfest celebration, which is basically the world's biggest fair—sixteen days of music, beer, lederhosen, and Bavarian hats called *Tirolerhüte*, which are decorated with goat fur.

"I think that's when I first started hating oom-pah music," said Tommy. "It was very, very loud, and my ears were very, very small."

Finally, on day four of our lock-in, Beck and I hatched an escape plan.

We decided we'd do what kids all over the world do best.

We'd drive the grown-ups crazy.

"We're the Kidds," I declared to our guards. "We've lived our whole lives on the open sea or in the wilds of the jungle. We are used to big skies, fresh air, and salty water. We're Wild Things. We go wherever the wind blows and the adventure takes us."

"Most days," said Tommy, "I don't even wear socks."

"He seldom uses deodorant, either," added Storm.

"Chyah. I'm a free bird."

"Let us out," I started chanting. "Let us out! Let us out!"

Soon, my sibs were joining in. "Let us out! Let us out!"

We added some of those thunderous "we will, we will rock you" hand claps and foot stomps.

"Let us out!" *Clap-clap-stomp!* "Let us out!"

"Enough!" cried Franz Hans. "Put on your socks and coats. We are going out for a walk!"

"Are you certain this is wise?" asked one of the other goons.

"Twelve armed guards against four foolish children?" Franz Hans said with a chuckle. "What could possibly go wrong?"

CHAPTER 59

When we reached a street called Sonnenstrasse, very close to the City Kino

movie theater, Beck and I initiated part two of our escape plan: Twin Tirade No. 501.

"Okay, Bickford," said Beck, coming to a dead stop. "Where exactly are we walking?"

"Nowhere. We're just on a walk."

"I want to go somewhere!"

"We are somewhere. We're out."

"*Out* is not a place."

"Yes, it is, Rebecca. And it's much better than 'in,' which is where we've been stuck for days."

Beck jabbed her fists into her hips and glared at me. I did the same thing. We were nose to nose. Our guards looked a little nervous.

Then we made them frantic. We went full, out-of-control, nutzoid bonkers on each other. People stopped to stare. A pair of police officers, too.

To make Twin Tirade No. 501 even more special, Storm and Tommy joined in—just like I told them they should.

"We want to see the movie!" shouted Storm.

"I want Milk Duds," hollered Tommy. "And Goobers."

"Junior Mints!" shouted Beck.

"Raisinettes," cried Storm. "And Twizzlers. A box the size of a small suitcase!"

"Haribo Gold-Bears," I said, because I understand they are very popular at German flicks.

"Hey, look," said Tommy, launching into the dialogue I had scripted for him. "There is. A movie theater. Let's all go. To the movies."

Yep. Tommy still memorized lines in chunks.

"We want the movie," the four of us chanted. "We want the movie!"

The police officers moved a few steps closer. Franz Hans looked even more nervous.

Herr Keplernicht was grinning like a lunatic at the police, who were starting to eye him suspiciously.

"Hurry, children," said Franz Hans, ushering us into the cinema's lobby. "We don't want to miss a minute of the movie."

All sixteen of us marched into the City Kino. That's right. It was part of our plan.

Because City Kino was the name of the movie theater printed on all those ticket stubs we found in the safe house.

CHAPTER 60

I nside the theater, Tommy spent a little more time than usual at the concession stand.

A very pretty German girl, maybe a year older than him, was working behind the counter, scooping up popcorn in red-and-white-striped cardboard tubs.

"Your eyes are amazing, do you know that?" he told her. "You should never shut them, not even at night."

The girl used her amazing eyes to give Tommy a look. "That's a line from a movie."

"Chyah. Ever heard it before?"

"*Ja.* I've heard them all. Over and over. I work in a movie theater, remember?"

"Your film is about to start," said the girl behind the counter, handing Tommy his tub of hot, buttered popcorn.

"Hey, this is a lot of popcorn. What would you say if I asked you to share it with me?"

"Nothing," said the girl. "Because I can't talk and laugh at the same time."

Beck and I giggled. Sorry, but the German girl was funny, sharp, and quick. We'd never seen one of Tommy's flirtation targets shoot him down so fast. We loved this girl.

"Well," said Tommy, not giving in. "The movie lasts like two hours. Plenty of time for you to change your mind."

"True," said the girl. "But not nearly enough for the brain surgeons to replace yours."

Even Storm laughed at that one.

But Tommy would not admit defeat. He kept trying to charm his way into the German girl's heart. "I think fate brought us together."

"Really? I was thinking it was just bad luck."

Now Streckting's armed goons were grinning and elbowing one another. They were enjoying Tommy's crash and burn, too. The little romantic comedy in the movie theater lobby was an excellent diversion. Our captors were too busy laughing at Tommy to keep their eyes on Beck as she scribbled a quick note on one of the ticket stubs she'd brought with her from the safe house.

Finally, Tommy took his popcorn and, trying his best to keep looking cool, sauntered away from the concession stand.

"Don't worry, guys," he said to the guards. "She's just playing hard to get."

While Franz Hans and the guards mumbled stuff like *"Er ist so ein Versager!"* (which, I think, meant Tommy was, officially, Germany's biggest loser), Beck passed her note to the girl behind the candy counter.

We hurried into the theater to watch *The Book Thief.*

But, if our plan worked, we wouldn't be around to see how the movie ended.

CHAPTER 61

The movie was in German without English subtitles, but Storm translated for us in a frantic whisper.

"Rudy Steiner just said, 'You're stealing books? Why?' And Liesel said, 'When life robs you, sometimes you have to rob it back.'"

"*Ja*," said Franz Hans, sitting in the row behind us. "Exactly! Life robs you, you rob it back. I like this Liesel...."

That's when the whole theater went dark.

No lights, no movie projector. Nothing.

"Hey! Who turned out the lights?" I heard Franz Hans shout while the four of us ducked down and scampered up our row of seats. The floor was kind of gummy—thanks to spilled soft drinks and tons of squished gummi bears—so we had to tread lightly to keep our shoes from making sticky-tacky noises and giving away our escape route.

Yep.

Our plan was now in motion.

CHAPTER 62

Beck's hunch had been correct.

We could totally trust the popcorn girl. She did everything we'd asked her to on that tiny ticket stub.

"Hurry," the girl said, slamming the exit door shut again.

"You have to come with us," I said.

"We don't know our way around Germany," added Beck. "And only Storm speaks the language."

"We'll give you a big reward," I offered. "Just as soon as we find the treasure we're hunting."

"Reward?" scoffed the girl. "I do not live my life

in the hope of being rewarded for doing what I know is right."

"Well," said Tommy, wiggling his eyebrows, "I've lived mine in the hope of meeting you."

"Some boys never change," muttered the girl.

"Wait a second," said Beck. "You've met Tommy before?"

"Let us just say I know your parents. And I would do anything for them."

"Um, have you seen our dad lately?" I asked.

We heard voices inside the theater: "I think they went this way! Or maybe that way! Ouch! I stubbed my toe."

We also heard a bunch of "oofs" and "get off my foot." Guess the lights were still out in the theater, and the musclemen were stumbling and bumbling into one another.

"Come," said the German girl. "This way. We can borrow a car I saw parked in the alley."

She darted up the slick cobblestone street. We followed her.

Since we ran out about halfway through the

movie, I've never actually seen all of *The Book Thief*. But this brave and feisty German girl reminded me of Liesel Meminger—a character I absolutely loved when I read the book.

I loved the German girl even more when I saw the car. It belonged to one of the goons in Franz Hans's crew.

It was a Mercedes sedan with room enough for five.

That meant it would be fast. Very, very fast.

CHAPTER 63

The German girl was behind the wheel as we sped up the autobahn, a multilane super-highway that winds its way across Germany like a snake.

Tommy was up front, riding shotgun. He was also hanging on to the overhead handle for dear life.

"Uh, how fast are we going?" Tommy asked.

"One hundred and ninety-three point twelve kilometers an hour," said the girl.

"That's one hundred and twenty *miles* per hour," Storm translated.

"*Ja*. I want to put some distance between us and your friends."

"They're not our friends," I said. "They work for Dionysus Streckting, the most evil and physically repulsive villain in the world."

"I know all about Herr Streckting. Your father told me."

"And how exactly do you know our father?" asked Beck.

"We have been in contact for many years."

"Do you ever help him hunt for treasure?"

"Only one."

"So you know what he's looking for here in Germany?" I asked.

"*Ja*. The same thing my family and I have been searching for my whole life. Your parents and my parents have known each other for a very long time. They were very close when your parents lived in that apartment overlooking the Marienplatz."

I finally put two and two together. "You put the movie stubs and popcorn tubs in the apartment."

"And my Clue board game."

"You wanted us to find you!" said Beck.

"*Ja*."

"Well," said Tommy, still trying to flirt over the screaming Mercedes engine, "I know I've dreamed about finding *you*."

The girl stomped on the gas pedal.

The car lurched forward like a rocket ship.

I think we were doing 140, maybe 150 mph.

Tommy wasn't flirting anymore. In fact, he had his eyes closed. His cheeks sort of flapped and wobbled on account of all the g-forces straining against his face.

"Excuse me," said Storm from the backseat, struggling to be heard over the fine whine of German engineering. "Why have you spent your whole life looking for one treasure?"

"Let's just say it is personal. I owe it to my family."

She cut the steering wheel hard to the right.

We swerved across two lanes and zoomed off an exit ramp.

She downshifted, eased on the brakes, and brought the Mercedes to a stop in a parking lot outside a prison-type building.

. She popped open her door.

"Come. I will show you what I mean."

CHAPTER 64

We were about ten miles northwest of Munich, facing some kind of memorial or museum.

A sculpture that looked like a barbed wire fence made out of bony bodies and limbs was erected above a brick wall with raised numbers spelling out the dates 1933–1945.

"Those are the years the Dachau Concentration Camp was in operation," explained the German girl. "It was the first such prison camp erected by the Nazis right after Hitler came to power. Thirty-two thousand deaths were documented right here at Dachau, many of them Jews. Some

of them members of my family. The Nazis took their homes, their money, their art, and, finally, their lives."

None of us said anything for a real long time.

I focused on a wall that bore NEVER AGAIN in five languages. It was like a prayer that something as horrible as genocide—the deliberate and systematic extermination of a whole race or religious group—would never be allowed to show its ugly face on earth again.

Tommy finally broke the silence.

"You know, guys, being here, seeing this memorial, makes what we're doing way more important."

"Kind of puts everything in perspective," said Storm. "We can't let Streckting and weird Uncle Timothy steal all that stolen art."

"We have to find it all first and keep them from getting their hands on it," I said.

"And give it all back to its rightful owners," added Beck.

"Totally," said Tommy.

"I'm glad to hear you say that," said the German

girl. "Because my family, with the help of your parents, has been tracking down the missing degenerate art for decades."

"Have you seen our dad lately?" I asked.

"No. But we have been in communication. He told me you might be coming to the safe house where your family once protected mine. So I planted the clues...."

"Whoa, wait a second," said Tommy, squinting at the German girl like, all of a sudden, he had X-ray vision. "Are you Petra? Petra Pichelsteiner?"

The German girl finally smiled. "Yes, Thomas. It is good seeing you again."

Tommy sort of blushed. "Wow. You've grown up. I mean, you used to be this little girl. Now you're, well, like I said—you're all grown up."

"Shall I take that as a compliment?"

"Definitely."

"Thank you. Now then, fellow treasure hunters, if you don't mind, we have much work to do."

CHAPTER 65

"So where do we go now?" said Beck, sounding frustrated. "We're all out of clues."

We were standing in the parking lot of the Dachau Memorial, clustered around our "borrowed" Mercedes.

"Plus," Beck continued, "by now, Franz Hans and his flunkies have probably noticed that one of their henchman-mobiles is missing."

"No way are we going back to the safe house," I said.

Petra shook her head. "Too risky."

"And if it's risky," said Tommy, "the safe house isn't actually 'safe' anymore, huh, Petra?"

Petra rolled her eyes. "Way to use your noodle, Thomas."

"Thanks," he said, puffing up his chest a little and shooting Petra a wink. "Dad told Uncle Timothy, who told Herr Streckting, that I was the smartest Kidd."

"When? Before any of your siblings were born?"

Tommy nodded. "I guess."

"You guys?" said Beck. "We need to focus. Where did the Nazis hide the stolen art?"

"We're missing something," mumbled Storm.

"What do you mean?" asked Petra.

"So far," Storm explained, "Mom and Dad's clues, no matter how absurd or abstract, have pointed us in the right direction."

"Following Dad's trail of bread crumbs to Munich is how we found you," I said to Petra.

"Totally," said Tommy. "Best. Clues. Ever."

Petra continued ignoring him.

"Okay," I said, "I have a dumb idea."

"At this point," said Beck, "I'll take it."

"What if we contacted Uncle Timothy?"

Tommy raised his hand. "Um, Bick? Uncle T. has gone over to the dark side of the Force."

"I know. But maybe *he* knows something he doesn't know he knows."

"Huh. Just like me."

"It's worth a shot," said Storm with a shrug. She fiddled with her iPad.

"What are you doing?" asked Petra.

"Disabling location services. We can Skype Uncle T. With the GPS switched off, he won't be able to pinpoint where we are."

"Unless," said Beck, "he checks out the background and sees the Dachau Memorial."

"Good point," said Storm. "Tommy? You make the call. But do it from inside the car."

"I'll handle the camera work," I offered. "I can make sure Uncle T. doesn't see anything except Tommy's face and the plush leather upholstery of this very sporty Mercedes."

I took the iPad from Storm. Tommy started primping for his on-camera screen time.

CHAPTER 66

Tommy slipped behind the wheel of the Mercedes.

I climbed into the passenger seat to frame up the shot for his video chat.

"You ready?" I asked.

"Chyah," said Tommy.

Petra rapped her knuckles on the driver-side window.

"One second, Bick." Tommy powered down his window. "Hi. Do you, uh, want to insult me again or something?"

"No," said Petra, with a soft smile. *"Viel Glück!"*

"Is that the sound a German duck makes?"

Petra laughed. "No, Thomas. It means *good luck.*"

"Oh. Okay. Thanks."

Tommy smiled at Petra. Petra smiled at him.

Beck cleared her throat. "You guys? Can we save the smilefest for later?"

"Right," said Tommy. "Hold that thought, Petra." He powered his tinted window shut. "Okay, Bick. Make the call."

I tapped the Video Call button.

Uncle Timothy answered almost immediately.

He did not look happy.

"Uncle T!" Tommy said with a big smile. "How's it hanging?"

"You kids made a big mistake. But it's not too late to come back."

"Right." Tommy asked, "Have you guys freed Mom yet?"

"That information is classified, Thomas. Top secret."

"No way," said Tommy. "You're not working for the CIA anymore."

"What? Who told you that?"

"The most interesting and physically repellent man in the world."

"Streckting said that about me?"

"Yep."

"Look, Thomas." Uncle T. sounded nervous. He lowered his voice. "This thing is about to run off the rails. Your 'aunt Bela' has gone rogue.

"Bela Kilgore has made unauthorized contact with your mother's kidnappers in Cyprus," said Uncle Timothy.

"Unauthorized? By who?"

"Dionysus Streckting."

"Wait a second. Wasn't that what she was supposed to do? Her mission was to deliver the Ming vase to the bad guys in Cyprus...."

"She didn't wait for our call!"

"So? Did she make the deal? Is Mom safe now?"

"That's irrelevant."

"Uh, no it's not."

"Yes, Thomas, it is. Unless you children find the hiding place for all that degenerate art, Dionysus Streckting *will* make a call. When he does, no way will Aunt Bela be able to protect your mother, wherever they are. Not for long. They'll both wind up dead."

"Well, to be honest, Uncle T., we've sort of hit a dead end on the art treasure hunt front. Can you give us some kind of clue? Even a semiclue would help. Or a hint. A hint would be awesome."

"Where are you, Tommy? Franz Hans and his people are looking for you. They say you 'disappeared.'"

"No, we didn't. That would mean I was invisible right now."

"Where are you?"

"Like I said—in a car."

"Don't play games with me, son."

"Yo. I am definitely not your son because you are definitely nothing like my dad."

Uncle Timothy looked steamed. Then he started humming that tune Mom hummed in her video.

"Such a silly song," he said with icicles dangling off his words. "What if that little lullaby is the last any of us ever hears from your mother? What if she and your father end up dead because of your stupidity, Thomas? So one last time—tell me where you are. Now!"

Tommy narrowed his eyes. "You don't scare me, Uncle T. Not anymore. You're nothing but a coward and a traitor."

Uncle Timothy grinned.

And kept on humming.

"Kill him," said Tommy.

"Um, I can't," I said. "He isn't really here. Besides, I'm not sure killing Uncle Timothy will change—"

Tommy waved his hand at the iPad. "I meant kill the call."

I tapped the End Call icon.

Knuckles rapped on the glass again. Tommy rolled down his window.

"Way to go, Thomas," said Petra, another smile brightening her face.

"Huh?"

"We heard everything out here. And..." Petra nodded toward Storm. "Apparently, your strange uncle Timothy *did* know something he didn't know he knew."

CHAPTER 67

"Petra's right," proclaimed Storm. "I figured it all out."

"Awesome," said Tommy.

"Way to go!" Beck and I added.

"So what exactly did you figure out?" asked Tommy.

"Everything. Uncle Timothy gave us the final clue. I know where the missing degenerate art is hidden."

"Really?" I said. "Because all I heard him do was threaten Tommy and hum Mom's lullaby."

"Which, I realized, is a few notes off from the one Dad used to hum to me, the difference being that Mom's lullaby is based on Plato's musical code."

"Play-Doh?" said Tommy. "I had a Play-Doh Fun Factory once. Used to make those spaghetti string things and eat 'em."

Petra gave Tommy a quizzical look. "Thomas? I believe your sister is referring to Plato, the ancient Greek philosopher."

"Oh. Riiiight. *Plato.*"

"Correct," said Storm, tucking her hands behind her back and pacing around the parking lot like an absentminded college professor. "The song Mom was humming in her video was actually a coded message. By mocking it, Uncle Timothy was unwittingly resending us Mom's message. One we'd all missed before."

"Wait a second," I said. "That lullaby was a secret message?"

"Yes. Based on Plato's musical code. The ancient Greeks believed music was the key to

mathematics and the cosmos. So Plato used Greek musical scales to give his works a hidden structure and then built layers of hidden meanings beneath that.

"First, we need to transcribe the musical notes in the lullaby to their mathematical equivalents," Storm said as she finished scribbling a very long and extremely complex mathematical formula on the front window of the Mercedes with her lip balm. "Now we take those numbers and, once again, using the same simple alphabet code we used to decipher the meaning of the Lucky Numbers on the back of our fortune cookie slips, we come up with...*N-E-U-B-I-B-E-R-G*!"

"Okay," said Beck. "I'll admit I was kind of excited there, sis. Right up to the point where Plato's secret musical code spelled out *nerdberger*."

Storm let out an exasperated sigh. "Not *nerdberger. Neubiberg*. Didn't you ever study German geography?"

"I did," said Petra. "Come on. Everybody back into the car."

"Where are we going?" I asked.

Storm let out another sigh. This one was even more exasperated. "Neubiberg!"

"It's a suburb nine kilometers south of Munich," explained Petra. "It used to have an airport, which the Nazis used as a Luftwaffe base during World War II. Messerschmitt fighter-bombers were stationed there."

"A Nazi air force base?" said Tommy. "That means Hitler could've flown his stolen art collection to Neubiberg on cargo planes."

"*Ja*," said Petra. "The Allies did not capture the air base until April 1945."

HURRY! THERE'S MORE ART WHERE THIS WAS STOLEN FROM!

"So let's go!" said Beck. "And Storm?"

"Yes?"

"I don't care what Dionysus Streckting says, you're definitely the real brains of this family!"

"Chyah," said Tommy. "Totally!"

CHAPTER 68

I t took us about forty minutes to drive from Dachau to Neubiberg.

It would've taken us less time if Petra had been behind the wheel instead of Tommy.

More proof we were on the right track?

When we pulled into Neubiberg, we saw the town's coat of arms.

Call me crazy, but the guy on the bottom looked an awful lot like Dad doing his birdman bit in Beijing.

(Wow. Beck just said that, despite my generous offer, she won't call me crazy. She said I actually uncovered a pretty decent clue. *For the first time ever.*)

"Okay," said Tommy as we cruised the suburban streets, "we're here. What are we looking for?"

"Sorry," said Storm. "Plato's musical code only told us *where* to look, not what to look for."

"Well, keep your eyes open, everybody," I said, because I could sense we were close to finding our treasure. When you're a treasure hunter, you just have a sixth sense about that sort of thing. "Don't ignore anything, no matter how trivial. Remember what Dad wrote in that text: 'The most important clues often seem small and insignificant.'"

"Your father said this to you?" asked Petra.

"Well, he texted us...."

Petra nodded. "He sent me the same message."

We drove up and down ordinary-looking German streets for what seemed like hours, all of us peering out the windows, looking for anything, no matter how small or insignificant.

Finally, as we were crawling along a side street, cruising past tidy hedgerows and bushy evergreen trees hiding whitewashed houses with terra-cotta roof tiles, Petra saw something.

"*Halt!*" she shouted. "Stop the car!"

Tommy slammed on the brakes.

We were in front of a building with the same kind of look as those ski chalets in Bavaria. Only this one was four stories tall and took up the whole block.

"That sign says it's a museum!" exclaimed Beck.

"Do you think they might have some of the stolen art on display?" I asked.

"Doubtful," said Storm. "However, they might be hiding it."

"I agree," said Petra.

"You do?" said Tommy eagerly. "Then I do, too."

Petra grinned. "And do you know why we stopped here, Thomas?"

"Um, because you told me to?"

"*Ja*. And because this is *Das Museum der Kleinen und Unbedeutenden Dinge*."

"Cool. And, uh, what does that mean?"

"It means we have found the place your father wanted us to find. It translates into *The Museum of Small and Insignificant Things*."

CHAPTER 69

The five of us ventured inside the museum for a look-see.

The place was open but empty. The air smelled like mildew and mothballs. The floors creaked under our feet. Display cases were filled with weird stuff, all of it extremely small and seriously insignificant.

We deposited five children's admissions into a coin box and started examining the so-called "art."

"This is all about the paper clip," said Beck, checking out one of the dusty glass boxes mounted on the dark walls. "Johan Vaaler, a Norwegian,

invented the paper clip and received a patent for his design from Germany in 1899...."

"Fascinating," said Storm, examining another of the miniature displays. "Here's an exhibit about toothpick flags...."

"Here's a bunch of cat hair balls," I reported. "Very historical—not to mention hysterical."

Suddenly a creepy old couple, decked out in matching Oktoberfest costumes, marched into the gloomy room.

"Vat are you children doing here?" asked the old man. He looked awfully grumpy for someone wearing embroidered shorts, suspenders, long socks, boots, and a feathered hat studded with pins.

"Checking out your teeny-tiny knickknacks," said Beck.

"Zose are not knickknacks!" the woman bellowed ferociously. "Zat is art!" The elderly woman was wearing what Storm called a "dirndl," a traditional Bavarian dress based on the historical costumes of Alpine peasants. To me, she sort of looked like the Swiss Miss girl after her cocoa curdled.

"Children are forbidden in this museum," said the woman.

"Excuse me, *alte Frau*," said Petra.

Storm put a hand alongside her mouth and translated: "Petra just called the old woman an 'old woman.'"

"If children are forbidden," Petra continued, "why do you have a children's admission price?"

The wrinkled old crone made a face like she'd

taken a whiff of spoiled sauerkraut. "The stupid *Bürgermeister* made us do it!"

"Well," said Tommy, "if he's the burger maestro, he must know what he is doing—and not just when he's flipping burgers. Come on, you guys, let's case this joint!"

"No! You can't! It is strictly forbidden!"

We split up and took off. Beck, Tommy, Petra, and I bounded up the steps. Storm tore down a hallway on the main floor. The spooky old museum curators couldn't keep up with any of us.

It was like a huge art heist in the making. (I guess that's why Beck drew us all like cat burglars, even though I had no interest in swiping the museum's hair ball collection.)

"Petra and I will take the second floor," said Tommy. "You guys head up to three."

"Let us know if you find anything!" called Petra as Beck and I climbed the staircase to the top floor, taking the steps two at a time.

Way off in the distance, I heard the old couple hollering "stop" and "children are filthy insects" a few times. But they never threatened to call the police. Probably because they didn't want the police nosing around in their business.

Maybe the creepy old couple was hiding something big and *major* in their "small and insignificant" museum.

CHAPTER 70

B eck and I searched every nook and cranny of the museum's top floor.

All we found were more display cases crammed with small, useless stuff. Pushpins. Spools of thread. Those tiny toothpaste tubes the dentist always gives you. The cheap, itty-bitty toys that tumble out of vending machines inside plastic balls.

Nothing that would be considered master-pieces by anyone but the loony couple who worked here.

It was enough to drive a pair of twins into another tirade.

We stopped hollering when Beck stepped on something pale and squishy.

"Gross," said Beck. "What was that?"

"Who knows? Maybe cockroaches are considered works of art in this ridiculous museum. They're small enough."

As Beck was examining the sole of her shoe, something struck her.

"Do you think Dionysus Streckting got here before us? What if he's here right now?"

Okay. That freaked me out. Slightly.

Because it was a definite possibility.

So Beck and I continued our search of the third floor on tiptoe. We both kept expecting some kind

of Bavarian bogeyman to pop out of the shadows to make us listen to opera or eat sauerbraten again.

We crept into every room.

We examined every exhibit, every display.

We found nothing.

Except a sign alerting us that the museum doors closed at 1800, European for 6 PM.

We had five minutes before the grouchy German couple could officially kick us out.

"Let's go find the others," Beck suggested.

We darted quietly down the steps to the second floor.

As we did, I could hear the old man announcing, "Zis museum closes in five minutes! Any meddlesome children, infants, or toddlers found on the premises after hours shall be dealt with most severely. Do I make myself clear?"

We found Tommy, Petra, and Storm huddled in a dark corner behind a cabinet displaying "The History of Lapel Pins."

"What do we do?" I whispered.

"We keep quiet," said Petra. "And we hide."

"The museum is closing," said Beck.

"So?" said Storm. "We're the Kidds. There are no 'closing hours' when we have more to explore. We're Wild Things, remember?"

We all nodded.

"This way," whispered Tommy, tapping the wall.

A panel sprang open.

"Petra and I found a secret staircase. It leads to the basement."

CHAPTER 71

Through the basement's sidewalk-level casement windows, we could see the odd old couple locking the museum's front door.

"Are you certain the nosy American brats left?" asked the sourpuss old woman.

"*Ja*, Helga. The German girl, too."

"You are positive about this, Ludwig?"

"*Ja*. Now can we please go home? My lederhosen itch. My stomach growls."

"If you are wrong…"

"I am not! Come. We are late for supper."

What do you know? Ludwig was lying to Helga because he didn't want to miss his potato pancakes and sauerkraut. Maybe they'd be chowing down on some of that spreadable sausage stuff, too.

"We give them five minutes to make sure they're gone," said Tommy. "Then we tear this basement apart."

"But we do so carefully," said Petra. "The art we are looking for is extremely valuable. Especially to the families it was stolen from."

"Chyah," said Tommy. "So remember, you guys: Nice to touch, nice to hold, but if you break it, consider it sold."

Petra arched an eyebrow.

"Sorry," said Tommy. "I saw that in an antiques shop once. Dad and I were selling them a couple cannonballs. It sort of stuck with me."

"Like bubble gum on his brain," added Storm.

The dank cellar was full of cardboard boxes and wooden crates. Were any of them hiding looted masterpieces? Was this where the Nazis had decided to stash their cache of stolen art treasures? Had they hidden millions of dollars of art in the damp and dingy basement of a two-bit German gewgaw museum?

Storm kept her eyes riveted on her dive watch.

"Okay," she announced. "Five minutes are officially up. It's time to hunt some treasure."

Five hours later, we still hadn't found anything bigger than a bread box.

"This makes no sense," I said, because I knew everybody else was thinking it. "Dad's clues all led us to this location."

"Do you guys think Dad sent us on a wild-goose chase?" asked Beck. "Has he just been putting us through some kind of treasure-hunting drill like he used to do on board *The Lost*?"

"No way," said Tommy. "Not for something this important."

"If it's so important," said Beck, "why isn't he here helping us?"

I quickly leaped to Dad's defense. "Because he's busy taking care of something even more important."

"Like what?"

"I dunno. Maybe he went to Cyprus to help Bela rescue Mom."

"And maybe you should stop dreaming."

"You guys?" said Tommy. "Chill."

"We need to work the clues again," said Petra. "Tell me everything that has happened on your quest."

With Petra as our audience, we started replaying our most recent Kidd family adventures. Before long, our stream of memories turned into a trickle of clues.

Dad's friend, the Chinese waiter Liu Wei, telling us, "Wise elders suggest that you move on to the bird's nest soup and squab."

Storm informing us that "squab" was just a fancy name for pigeon.

Dad, flapping like a bird, then disappearing on that Beijing street behind a flock of pigeons taking flight.

Dad's engineering plans for the S.C.U.B.B.A. drilling machine, written on the back of those folded origami—I mean *zhézhî*—birds, one of which, of course, was a paper pigeon.

The pigeon wallpaper in the safe house.

Dad's text message, the one where he suggested we send our Chinese handlers off to the pigeon races.

In that same text, he also wrote:

pigeons r key.

Pigeons are key...

CHAPTER 72

One second later Beck was hiking up her foot to check out the bottom of her shoe.

A gob of chunky white gunk was trapped inside the grooves of her right boot.

"That wasn't a cockroach I squished upstairs," she announced. "That was a squishy pile of pigeon poop. Third floor. Now!"

The five of us hustled up the ancient staircase and raced to the spot in front of the toy-car collection, where Beck had stepped in the bird mess.

Petra raised her hand in a signal.

We all froze.

She put a finger to her lips.

We didn't make a sound.

"Hear it?" Petra whispered, cupping her hand to her ear.

"Yeah," said Tommy. "It's you. Whispering."

"No. Listen again."

Now we were all tilting our heads sideways. Listening hard.

And we heard it.

A soft "coo-coo-coo" sound.

Roosting pigeons.

"The attic!"

Yep. We all said it together, again.

Then we took off running.

CHAPTER 73

Tommy spotted it first: One of those pull-down ladders in the ceiling.

He yanked it open.

The five of us scampered up the rickety rungs into the dirtiest, filthiest, featheriest attic imaginable. In the dim moonlight shining through a gable window, it looked like a dozen pillows had exploded. Ratty pigeon-down pillows.

Storm started sneezing. Petra started wheezing. I also heard a lot of heavy cooing and feather flapping.

Tommy tugged the chain on a naked lightbulb dangling just above the attic ladder.

Fluffy white flakes fluttered through the air.

Fifty, maybe sixty, pigeons were roosting in the rafters. Gray, white, speckled, black. The museum's attic was a huge pigeon coop where we'd ruffled a few feathers and stirred up quite a chorus of coos.

This flock wasn't very particular or tidy about its potty training, either. White goo drizzled down from the rafters and oozed across the floor like somebody had dropped a couple of gallons of gunky white paint. Some of the bird poop had, obviously, leaked through the floorboards and dribbled down to the museum room below where Beck stepped in it.

"Look," said Petra, gesturing toward a relatively un-bird-pooey corner. Old wooden crates lined up in tidy rows under the attic's eaves.

And they had Nazi swastikas painted on them.

"This is why your father sent us here," said Petra, sounding like she might cry. "We have finally found the missing art! We have fulfilled my family's mission."

"Bick?" Tommy said.

"Yeah?"

"Run back to the basement. I saw a couple crow-bars stowed in the corner."

"Aye, aye!"

I raced down to the basement to grab the tools.

It was time for the five of us to start ripping open Herr Hitler's packing crates.

CHAPTER 74

It was around midnight when we wrenched open
the first wooden box.

Inside was a Picasso.

"Easy with that crowbar," Petra coached Tommy.

"Sorry," he said, yanking down on the steel
rod in a way that definitely showed off his bulging
biceps.

SOMETIMES I DON'T KNOW MY OWN STRENGTH.

WHEW—I DO. YOU ARE ONE SMELLY DUDE, TOMMY.

We all laughed. It was probably the happiest night any of us had had in a long time.

We'd found the treasure! The same one Mom and Dad and Petra's parents had been hunting down for decades.

Sure, Dad was the one who had pegged its hiding place, but we kids were the ones who actually followed the "map" and "dug up" the treasure. For all five of us, there was no better feeling in the world.

So we kept going.

"Wow!" Beck gasped every time Tommy pried the squeaking nails out of a crate to reveal another hidden masterpiece.

"That's a Caravaggio!" she said. "A van Eyck! Monet! Matisse! Another Picasso. *Le pigeon aux petits pois!*"

"*The Pigeon with Green Peas?*" said Storm, skeptically translating Beck's French. "Seriously?"

"Yep," said Beck, grinning. "Looks like Dad knew all sorts of 'pigeons' were roosting up here in the attic!"

By three in the morning we had liberated enough stolen art to fill a museum wing, and we still had more packing crates to pry open.

We'd also shooed most of the pigeons out of the attic so they wouldn't, you know, "soil" anybody's long-lost masterpiece.

"So what do we do now?" Beck asked rhetorically. "Call the local police?"

Petra shook her head. "We may not be able to trust them. The old couple who run this so-called museum may not be the only ones who know its true purpose." She pulled out her cell phone. "On the other hand, Interpol, the International Criminal Police Organization, is extremely interested in Dionysus Streckting and his criminal activities. He's high on its list of 'Red Notices.' In fact, he might be Interpol's most wanted fugitive currently at large. Interpol is also quite concerned about finding the stolen Nazi art...."

"Good," said Tommy. "We'll call them. Whenever we ran across a dicey international legal question, Dad always trusted Interpol."

"Should we move the paintings first?" I suggested. "That creepy curator couple will be back. The pigeons, too."

Petra considered the idea. "We'd need a truck. Does your father have any CIA contacts here in—"

Before she could finish her question, we heard wood creaking.

But none of us was moving.

Someone else was climbing the rickety ladder to the attic!

CHAPTER 75

Somehow, Dionysus Streckting had found us. Uncle Timothy, Franz Hans Keplernicht, and assorted thuggish goons were with him.

All of them were armed.

"How'd you know where we were?" asked Tommy.

"Easy," said Streckting. "A local couple, Ludwig and Helga Schupfnudel, posted your pictures on the ultrasecret NefariousNet Listserv, which seamlessly links together evildoers all across the globe. The Schupfnudels were complaining about four American brats and a German girl nosing around their museum in Neubiberg. So, I…"

His jaw dropped.

He'd just seen the stack of paintings lined up under the attic eaves.

He clutched his chest. Caught his breath.

"You found it?"

"I told you these Kidd kids were good," bragged Uncle Timothy. "Our people in China will be very pleased."

"Indeed," said Streckting, rubbing his hands together, greedy raccoon–style. "After years of plotting, planning, and scheming, I am about to complete the largest art acquisition and sale in the history of the world! Am I not the most brilliant criminal genius in the universe?"

"And the most physically repellent," I said.

"Yeah," said Beck. "Fortunately, the stench of pigeon poop up here almost covers up the stench of your breath. *Almost.*"

Streckting raised a small pistol. "Step aside, children. That artwork belongs to me."

Petra raced to the paintings.

Tommy stretched out his arms to shield her and block Streckting's advance.

More weapons were racked and raised.

"Don't be a fool, Tommy," said Uncle Timothy. "Those old paintings aren't worth dying for."

"Yeah?" said Tommy. "Try telling that to the Jews who *lost their lives* when the Nazis put together this little collection. So back off, all of you. You know the rules of salvage, Uncle Timothy."

"The rights to a treasure trove," said Storm, "are typically treated the same way as any other found property. The finder is the keeper."

"And the loser?" said Beck. "He is the weeper."

"So," I tossed in, "start weeping. Big-time."

"Children, children, children," said Streckting, lowering his pistol, which really didn't matter because all his thugs and even Uncle Timothy still had their weapons trained on us. "You have done your part. I will call my friends in Cyprus and tell them to set your mother free."

I played a hunch. "Aunt Bela already did that."

Streckting flinched. His eyes darted sideways to Uncle Timothy, who looked kind of queasy. Then Streckting composed himself. Smiled.

"Of course she did. I told her to. Now then, if you will all step aside. I really don't want my companions to splatter your gizzards all over my priceless paintings. It would be so difficult to wipe the artwork clean...."

Beck, Storm, and I bravely stepped forward to form a human wall with Tommy. We were protecting those paintings, no matter what.

Beck found more courage than the rest of us and launched into a solo tirade against Streckting, Uncle Timothy, and everybody else who ever tried to make money off the misery of others.

I don't think I've ever been prouder to be a twin. I was all choked up. Storm and Tommy, too. And Storm doesn't choke up easily.

But Streckting?

He was laughing hysterically.

"You Americans are so wonderfully naive. Especially you children. So innocent and pure. It disgusts me. Now move out of the way or, I swear, I will order my men to—"

That's when the unthinkable happened.

Petra turned around, reared back her arm, and punched her fist straight through the center of a Picasso.

CHAPTER 76

O kay. My mistake. It wasn't a Picasso.

It was a terrible portrait of Ludwig and Helga Schupfnudel holding their pet schnauzer that was probably painted by a local artist. A local artist who might be color-blind (unless schnauzers in Germany are really green).

What can I say? All ripping canvas sounds the same to me.

"Stand back," warned Petra, "or I will punch a hole in this Picasso pigeon painting next."

"You foolish little girl!" screamed Streckting. "Do you know how much money such a teenaged temper tantrum would cost me?"

"Over one hundred and fifty-five million dollars," said Uncle Timothy. "According to my preliminary intel, that's how much a billionaire spent for a single Picasso painting back in 2013."

"The Chinese will give me more!" sputtered Streckting.

"Roger that," said Uncle Timothy. "The high cultural minister has a very generous budget for his new museum. Of course, my sales commission would've been—"

"Silence!" Streckting screamed, spewing wet gobs of spittle across the room.

"We don't care about the money," said Tommy.

"And you're not selling this art to anybody," added Beck.

"That's where you are wrong, little girl," said Streckting. "There are, what, four of you?"

"Five," said Petra.

"Five. Five children. Unarmed infants."

"Actually," said Tommy with an ear wiggle, "Petra and I are kind of like young adults."

"*I don't care!* Do you seriously think you are any match for *me*, Dionysus Streckting? I am the most fascinating and dangerous man in the entire world. Interpol has me at the top of its most wanted list and it doesn't even know that *I* was the one who embezzled all that money in Switzerland last winter. But can it stop me? Ha! *No!* Can it even find me, even though it spent millions of dollars and thousands of hours in its foolish manhunt? *No!* Ha! I laugh at those Interpol idiots. Ha-ha-ha! I spit on their shiny Interpol badges...*ptooey*! So, if I am not afraid of the big bad international police, why should I be afraid of you inconsequential children when I can simply shoot you, one by one, and take what is rightfully mine?"

"You know," said Tommy, "you raise some pretty good questions. Can we have a few minutes and get back to you with our answers?"

Streckting doubled over with laughter.

"Tommy, Tommy, Tommy. The 'brains' of the family. Ha-ha-ha. You kill me. No wait. Strike that. *I* kill *you*. Yes. You will be the first Kidd to have his imbecilic brains blown out of his skull!

It will be a very entertaining, very amusing spectacle. One that I, Dionysus Streckting, will enjoy watching."

Now Streckting turned to Uncle Timothy with a sinister grin. "Timothy?"

"Yes, sir?"

"I trust your gun is loaded?"

"Affirmative. Standard operating procedure."

"Good. Will you kindly do the honors of killing Tailspin Tommy? One bullet between the eyes should do the job nicely."

Uncle Timothy hesitated. For, like, half a second.

"Is this a mission-crucial command?" he asked.

"Yes!"

"Very well."

Uncle Timothy raised his pistol.

Beck, Storm, and I rushed to help our big brother, but were held back by Streckting's goons. We begged Uncle Timothy to put his gun down, but he just ignored our desperate pleas.

I closed my eyes. I couldn't bear to watch.

CHAPTER 77

B ut just as Uncle Timothy was about to pull the trigger...

"Halt," said Petra, very calmly, especially considering the fact that Uncle Timothy still had his pistol pointed at Tommy's skull. "I have a better idea."

And she showed Streckting her cell phone.

The call screen was glowing.

"Those 'idiots' at Interpol would like to speak to you." Petra was looking grim as she held up her phone.

Streckting? He was foaming at the mouth. And the ears.

"Killing those children would be a very bad idea, Dionysus," said a tinny voice coming out of Petra's speakerphone.

"What? Who are you?"

"Senior Superintendent Aiden Buchholz, Interpol Wiesbaden. Thank you for alerting us to your current position as well as adding 'mastermind of global art smuggling league' and 'embezzler of Swiss funds' to your arrest warrant. At this point, I would strongly advise against adding the grave charges of harming the Kidds or Frau Pichelsteiner to that list."

Outside, I could hear the sound of approaching sirens.

"Our friends at the Munich Police Department have been very cooperative and are currently on their way to your location, which Frau Pichelsteiner's cell phone GPS chip has identified quite nicely for us. We always suspected that the 'miniatures museum' in Neubiberg was somewhat sketchy."

Now I heard the thump-thump-thump of rotors hovering over the museum.

Streckting was glaring up at the filthy attic rafters. He heard it, too.

"The Munich police are even letting us borrow their *Hubschrauber*," said the Interpol officer on Petra's phone.

"That's German for *helicopter*," said the ever-helpful Storm.

Streckting's henchmen started fidgeting and eyeballing their escape hatch—the narrow opening in the floor for the attic ladder.

"And thank you, Herr Streckting," Senior Superintendent Buchholz continued. "We were able to quite clearly record your entire confession.

Your monologue has made the prosecutor's job much easier. By the way, is Mr. Quinn with you? Mr. Timothy Quinn? Our American friends at the Central Intelligence Agency would like to have a few words with him as well. Preferably in a top secret location..."

"No," Streckting snarled, his sudsy mouth foaming like a washing machine with way too much detergent. "I will not let those idiots at Interpol lock me away for three hundred years!"

He shoved Uncle Timothy and Franz Hans out of the way and scampered down the rickety attic ladder first.

"Jeder für sich!" shouted Franz Hans.

This time, Petra handled the translation: "That means *every man for himself.*"

"That's been *your* motto all along," I said to Uncle Timothy. "Hasn't it?"

"Putting us in that horrible New York City prep school," fumed Storm.

"Selling off our only home, *The Lost*," added Tommy.

"Making us give both of our Ming vases to the

Chinese instead of sending one to Cyprus to rescue Mom," said Beck.

I shook my head. "And we thought you were Dad's friend."

Uncle Timothy whipped off his mirrored sunglasses. His eyes were filled with panic.

"Your father turned me in."

"Well, duh," said Tommy. "That's what the good guys usually do."

"*Ja,*" said Petra. "They rat on the rats."

The helicopter and sirens sounded like they were right outside.

Uncle Timothy's eyeballs shot back and forth a few times.

Then he tapped his stupid Bluetooth earpiece. "Initiate the extraction package."

He dashed over to the ladder and scurried down.

"Been fun, Kidds. Gotta go."

And Uncle Timothy disappeared.

CHAPTER 78

The Munich police lost Dionysus Streckting in all the confusion but nabbed several of his henchmen and turned them over to Interpol.

Uncle Timothy, Franz Hans Keplernicht, and one other goon also slipped through the police dragnet.

"Don't worry," said Interpol Senior Superintendent Buchholz, "the four still at large won't get very far. Every law enforcement agency in the world is searching for them."

Later that morning, when they arrived to open up their sham museum, Ludwig and Helga Schupfnudel were also promptly arrested.

Apparently, in the years since the end of the Second World War, the cranky old couple had, from time to time, sold off some of the priceless paintings to unscrupulous buyers around the world in order to raise the money they needed to keep their bogus museum front operational.

One of those buyers was Ms. Portia Macy-Hudson from Charleston, South Carolina—a kooky black-market art dealer whom we worked with a few months ago. It was through her that Dad had learned where the artwork was hidden. I guess he didn't have time to find the stash himself before he realized Uncle Timothy had gone rogue.

The Schupfnudels—who fell in love when they both were stationed at that Luftwaffe air base—had twisted dreams of a new Hitler coming to power and wanted to share in the new "Führer's" glory by becoming his degenerate-art custodians. Now the cranky curators would be spending the rest of their lives in jail cells, where the only art they'd see would be sculptures carved out of soap.

Buchholz and his team from Interpol took custody of the stolen Nazi art.

"We will work with the appropriate international agencies to ensure that the art is carefully restored and then returned to the original owners or their heirs."

The news of our amazing discovery in that German attic was splashed all across the globe. Kidd Family Treasure Hunters Inc. had its sterling reputation boosted even higher. We were back in business, big-time!

Of course, we still hadn't completed our primary treasure-hunting goal.

We still hadn't found Mom or Dad.

And we hadn't even heard from either one of them in days.

CHAPTER 79

Then guess what happened?

To celebrate the Kidd family's awesome treasure-hunting skills, the city of Munich—just like the city of Beijing—threw us a parade.

And, of course, Petra Pichelsteiner was on our horse-drawn float with us.

The *Bürgermeister* (or mayor) of Munich was riding with us, so Tommy kept asking him if his fries were as good as the ones at Mickey D's. The mayor just smiled and let Tommy borrow his binoculars so he could check out all the pretty girls screaming at him along the parade route.

The rest of us spent our time waving at the cheering crowds. It seemed everybody in Germany was happy to see the degenerate art being returned to its rightful owners.

The stories we heard of families being reunited with their treasures made Beck and Petra cry.

Okay, I might have sniffled a little, too.

As we neared a bridge crossing the choppy Isar River, which runs through Munich, Tommy turned to Petra and cranked up his charm to full blast.

"Now that it's all done," he said suavely, "I think you'll agree—treasure hunting sure brings people closer together."

"Thomas?"

"Yes?"

"You sound like a bad greeting card."

"I'm just saying that, maybe, you and me—we should do this again."

"What? Almost get killed by a psychopathic criminal mastermind like Herr Streckting?"

"Chyah."

"Let's not and say we did."

"Cool. Works for me."

Our horse-drawn wagon was clomping across the bridge when Beck and I both saw something absolutely, unbelievably incredible sailing downstream.

We both gasped and shouted, "*The Lost!*"

CHAPTER 80

S omeone had chopped down our beloved sailing ship's masts, but it was definitely *The Lost*.

Even though that would be impossible, because we had lost *The Lost* months ago when Uncle Timothy made us auction it off in New York.

"Who was at the helm?" cried Beck as the ship disappeared under the bridge.

"I couldn't see!"

"Me neither."

I elbowed Storm, then Tommy.

"Not now, Bick," said Tommy. He was giving Petra another one of his looks.

"You guys?" shouted Beck. "Downstream!"

The boat had come out the other side.

It was definitely *The Lost*—its name was even painted across the stern.

Suddenly, all four of our iPhones started buzzing again.

It was a text message. From Dad!

> Sorry I missed all the fun.
> I was busy.
> In Cyprus.

Boo-yah! I was right again. Dad hadn't simply abandoned us to Dionysus Streckting and his German goon squad. He hadn't been helping us in Germany because he'd been dealing with those other goons—the ones down in Cyprus who kidnapped Mom!

"Uh-oh," said Storm, who'd been looking *upriver*. "He's baaaack."

The rest of us whipped around and saw what Storm had just seen.

Maybe a mile upstream, three sleek black Jet Skis were flying down the river, bouncing across one another's wakes. The sun glinted off a pair of mirrored sunglasses behind the throttle of the Jet Ski in the middle.

Even from a mile away, we knew who it was.

Uncle Timothy.

Beck grabbed the binoculars from Tommy and whirled around to check out the decks of *The Lost*.

"It's definitely Mom and Dad," said Beck. "And Aunt Bela, too!"

I couldn't believe it. Had we gone through all this to find our parents and save their lives, only to lose them both to Uncle Timothy, the traitorous double-triple agent? Because, even as far away as they were, I could see that the three men on the Jet Skis were all armed with very heavy weaponry.

"Uncle Timothy is going to kill Dad!" I hollered. "For turning him in to Interpol and the CIA!"

"Not on my watch!" shouted Tommy.

Tommy dashed up to the front of the horse-drawn cart and leaped into the driver's seat to take the reins.

Tommy snapped the leather leads. The humongous, Clydesdale-sized horses took off. So did our float. We all hung on to the nearest flower garlands so we wouldn't fall off the wagon.

"Where are we going?" Petra shouted at Tommy.

"To save Mom and Dad!"

CHAPTER 81

Tommy cracked the reins again, and our two-horsepower family wagon flew across the bridge and down to the paved walkway lining the shores of the Isar River.

Out in the water, I noticed *The Lost* was losing speed and turning about.

"Why are they slowing down?" I hollered.

"The hydroelectric plant!" shouted Storm, who, obviously, had memorized a river map of Munich, too. "There's a big dam and a waterfall hidden behind the ship."

"Boats!" cried Beck, pointing to a boat-rental place on the riverbank near us.

"Whoa!" Tommy pulled back on the reins.

Beck, Tommy, Petra, and I jumped off the wagon and ran to grab a boat.

We could hear the whine of Uncle Timothy's churning Jet Ski coming closer.

"Our sister will pay!" Beck shouted to the guy in the boat-rental kiosk as she raced past.

Beck and I hopped into a rowboat while Tommy and Petra grabbed a paddleboat. Storm stayed on shore to pay our rental fees.

"We'll never be able to stop three Jet Skis with a stupid rowboat!" shouted Beck.

"Never say never!" I shouted back.

"I just did!"

"I know. I heard you."

We shoved off and rowed out into the swiftly moving stream.

Behind us, I heard grunting and groaning. Tommy and Petra had made a very bad decision. They were getting nowhere fast pumping the bicycle pedals in that paddleboat.

It was up to me and Beck to—somehow—save Mom and Dad.

"Stroke!" Beck hollered from the bow of the boat, because I was the one sitting backward in the stern and doing all the rowing. "Stroke!"

I pulled with all my might.

I heard the *clink-clink-clink* of a tumbling chain. *The Lost* must've just dropped anchor.

"They've brought the ship to a full stop," reported Beck. "It's a sitting duck!"

I saw the three Jet Skis thundering downstream.

"And here come the duck hunters!"

CHAPTER 82

The screaming Jet Skis were heading straight for *The Lost.*

Metal flashed in the sun.

The bad guys were raising their weapons.

"It's Dad!" shouted Beck from her vantage point up in the bow. "I can see him. It's really, really Dad! He's waving at us...."

And he was about to become "dead Dad" unless we did something.

Fast.

I yanked my left oar hard and spun us sideways, creating a small wooden barricade between .

the rapidly approaching Jet Skis and the broadside of *The Lost*.

As soon as I made my move, the trio of water-skimming motorcycles split up. Two went around our bow.

One went around our stern.

That's the guy I whacked with my paddle. Hard.

He went flying over the handlebars and into the river.

The goon was wearing a helmet, but I'm pretty sure it was Franz Hans.

One down, two to go.

"Take them out!" I heard Uncle Timothy scream as he goosed the throttle on his revving engine and fishtailed around and around in a circle.

The other Jet Ski swerved into an incredibly tight U-turn, sliced across the river, turned about, and was heading straight for our little dinghy when, with a burst of superhuman strength, Tommy and Petra pumped their pedals extra hard and steered their paddleboat so it was on course to collide with the Jet Ski. Then they both leaped out of their seats and abandoned ship.

The Jet Ski dude tried to pop a water wheelie and jump the empty paddleboat. But he should've practiced the stunt a few times before he attempted it.

His sputtering water scooter ended up in a barrel roll—spinning out of control. He and his AK-47 assault rifle belly flopped into the river.

Two down.

Only Uncle Timothy left.

"This is for Cairo!" I heard a woman shriek. I looked up and there was Aunt Bela. She and her jet pack had blasted off the deck of *The Lost* and were streaking like a bottle rocket straight at Uncle Timothy.

Uncle Timothy initiated a countermove. He yanked his handlebars hard to the left.

Bela missed her target and slammed into the water like a misguided missile.

Uncle Timothy laughed.

Well, he laughed until he realized he had circled directly into the powerful current dragging everything it could grab toward the dam's very narrow overflow. We're talking white-water-rapids-through-the-Grand-Canyon-style current.

Uncle Timothy tried to reverse engines.

But his souped-up Jet Ski wasn't as strong as the river when all its power and might were being squeezed down into one ten-foot-wide roaring rapid. There was nothing Uncle Timothy could do. The waterfall wanted him and wouldn't let him go.

"Noooo!" I heard him scream.

And then he disappeared over the edge in a thundering torrent of churning white water.

"Woo-hoo!" shouted Beck. "We did it."

I was about to "woo-hoo" with her.

Until I heard the helicopter.

CHAPTER 83

We looked up and saw him.
Dionysus Streckting.

"You stole the stolen art I should have stolen!"
he shouted like a madman from the cramped control pod of his teeny-tiny whirlybird. "For that, you
must pay!"

"Buzz off, Streckting," I heard Dad holler up to
the hornet-shaped helicopter.

"H-he is a h-horrible person!" said Aunt Bela as
she skittered across the water on her belly, pro-
pelled by her sputtering jet pack like some kind of
berserk skipping stone.

"Dad?" shouted Beck.

"No, Streckting!" cried Bela right before she bonked into the side of our rowboat with her crash helmet. She grabbed hold of the side of our dinky dinghy with her left hand and pressed a red button on the jet pack's handgrip controller with her right. The twin rockets finally cut out.

"Prepare to die!" hollered Dionysus Streckting from maybe fifty feet up above.

Speaking of rockets...

Streckting was standing up in his wobbly little helicopter with some kind of rocket-propelled grenade launcher propped on his shoulder.

He was aiming it down at the deck of *The Lost*.

"If I can't have all that art, then you can't, either! I am the most interesting and physically repellent man in the world. Who are you two? Nothing but a pair of insignificant garbage collectors, scouring the world for trash you dare call treasure!"

I'd heard enough.

"They're our parents!" I shouted.

"And they're way better than you, stinkface!" added Beck.

We looked at each other.

Then we looked down at Aunt Bela, who was treading water and unstrapping her jet pack.

Beck and I locked eyeballs again.

"You thinking what I'm thinking?" I said.

"Of course I am."

"I thought so."

Together, we reached down, grabbed hold of Aunt Bela's floating jet pack, and hauled it out of the water.

Then we aimed it up at Streckting's helicopter.

"On your mark," we said in perfect sync. "Get set. Go!"

I slammed the red button.

The two rockets whooshed to life.

The pilotless jet pack streaked skyward.

Bang!

"Direct hit!" shouted Tommy when our overgrown bottle rocket rammed into the side of Streckting's minichopper and sent him and his rocket-propelled grenade launcher tumbling out the door.

The most interesting and physically repellent man in the world splashed down in the river and started thrashing. I felt sorry for any fish in the vicinity, even though, come to think of it, Streckting sort of smelled like a fish. One that's been sitting in the sun. For a week.

Soon, the same rapids that had tugged Uncle Timothy over the lip of the dam dragged Dionysus Streckting over the waterfall, too. Still shouting and yelling, he disappeared in a bubbling rush of white water and went cascading over the edge!

CHAPTER 84

B eck and I swam like crazy toward *The Lost*.
So did Tommy and Petra.

I saw Storm cannonball off that riverbank and
start swimming so fast she sliced through the
water like a dolphin.

I couldn't believe it. We were just seconds away
from the greatest treasure in the world: our family
being a family again!

Beck and I reached the side of *The Lost* and
clambered up the waiting rope ladder to the deck.

"Mom! Dad!"

There were tears in our eyes. Theirs, too.

We squealed and screeched and hugged one another like crazy.

"I knew you were alive!" I said to Dad.

He squeezed me a little tighter. "Thanks for never giving up on me, Bick."

Beck and Mom finally broke out of their hug. "We missed you guys so much," they both said at the same time.

Tommy, Storm, and Petra climbed on board next. More hugs. More laughs. More amazing joy.

"I knew I could count on you all to take care of Streckting," said Dad, "while your mom and I dealt with those vase-loving thugs in Cyprus."

We had crossed all the major oceans and traipsed across four different continents in our quest to put our whole family back together. And it was all worth it for this one golden moment!

"Little help," we heard a voice peep off our starboard side.

Aunt Bela was dog-paddling alongside *The Lost*. Tommy hauled her onboard.

"Bela was working for us all along," said Mom. "She knew Uncle Timothy was up to no good."

Aunt Bela nodded proudly. "I was a *double-double* agent."

"I'm so sorry I had to abandon ship during that storm off the Caymans," said Dad. "But it was the only way we could stop Uncle Timothy."

"And you four?" said Mom. "You made us so proud. You handled everything the most despicable villains in the world threw at you."

"They're amazing!" added Petra. "Especially Thomas."

She went up on tiptoe and gave him a quick kiss on the lips.

"Wow!" said Tommy. "Petra Pichelsteiner, you are definitely all grown up!"

As for Uncle Timothy, the man who tried to ruin our family? Well, let's just say he didn't make it very far downstream and now he's going up the river.

(Yes, Beck, I think everybody knows *up the river* means he's going to a maximum-security federal penitentiary for a very, very long time.)

Dionysus Streckting, on the other hand, will continue being the world's most physically repellent man. But he'll be doing it in jail. Probably in solitary confinement.

Franz Hans was still at large. Not being the brightest bulb in the chandelier, he had a pretty good chance of eventually being caught.

Eventually, after all the hugging and kissing and laughing and crying, I started peppering Mom and Dad with questions.

"Where have you two been? How'd you get *The Lost* back? How'd you know Uncle Timothy was working with Dionysus Streckting? Did we miss any clues? You have to tell us *everything*!"

"Of course we do," said Dad, rubbing my hair just the way he used to.

"We have so, so much to tell you," said Mom with her heart-melting smile. "Our brave, wonderful children."

"But," said Dad, with a twinkle in his eye, "that's another story, for another day. Today? We need to shove off for Russia."

"What?" I said. "How come?"

"The Amber Room!" exclaimed Storm. "You guys know where it is?"

"Maybe," said Mom, with a small smile. "My kidnappers in Cyprus were very talkative."

"And since those louts will all be spending the next several decades behind bars," said Dad, "they really had no use for this."

He pulled a folded sheet of aged parchment paper out of his pocket.

Yep. You guessed it.

It was a treasure map.

The Kidd Family Treasure Hunters were officially back in business!

IT'S ROBOT BRAIN VS. ROBOT BRAWN IN A BATTLE FOR
THE HOUSE OF ROBOTS!

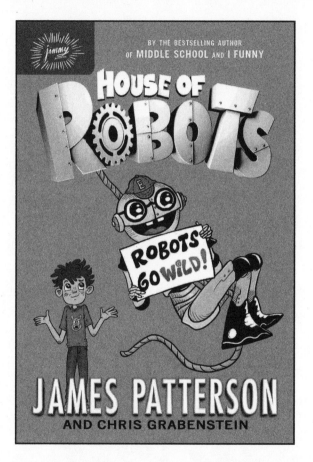

TURN THE PAGE FOR A SNEAK PEEK!
AVAILABLE FALL 2015

This is E.

When Mom first created him and said I had to take a robot to school with me every day, I thought E stood for *Error*—as in the biggest, hugest, most colossal mistake ever made. And, at first, he *did* make my life at school pretty nutso.

But then I found out why E had such enormous blue eyes.

Oh, right. Duh. The drawing is in black and white. But trust me, E's eyes are Blizzard Blue. The exact same color as my sister Maddie's.

See, Mom created E (she says the E stands for *Egghead*) to be Maddie's eyes, ears, and voice in Ms. Tracey's third-grade classroom at Creekside Elementary.

Why doesn't Maddie just go to school herself?

She can't. Not without getting really sick.

Now, I know a lot kids say going to school makes them sick. Especially on days when the cafeteria special is the beefy-cheesy nacho surprise.

But just going to school and breathing the air and being near other kids and all their germs could make my little sister seriously ill, because Maddie suffers from SCID, which is short for *severe combined immunodeficiency*. Basically, it means Maddie's body has a really hard time fighting off any kind of infection. If somebody coughs and forgets to cover their mouth, she could wind up in the hospital.

So what does it all mean? Well, Maddie hardly ever leaves home. In fact, she hardly ever leaves her room. That's why our family pet is a germ-free robot dog.

Why Mr. Moppenshine, the multiarmed multitasker, is constantly cleaning and disinfecting everything.

It's also why the only way for Maddie to actually go to school is for E to go there for her.

"You'd better hurry up, you guys! You don't want to be late."

That's my dad. Noah Rodriguez, the world-famous graphic novelist. He works from home, so he's never late.

"Your father is correct," says E. "We must not tarry."

Yep. E still sounds a little robot-ish. But he can't help it. Mom made him that way. Guess what she's making next? I'm not 100 percent sure, but I think it'll help Mr. Moppenshine scrub the toilets.

"Let's go, Sammy."

That's Maddie, speaking through E, just like she'll do at school. When the first bell rings, Maddie will run E from the nifty control pod set up in her room.

I just hope she doesn't make E do something super girly, like scream about boy bands or spin like a ballerina.

At least, not while I'm around.

Oops.

I think E and I are going to be a little tardy for school today.

When we step out the back door and hurry down the steps—something, by the way, that E does incredibly well for a robot—there's a whole mob of people waiting for us in the driveway.

I guess word has spread about what E's been doing for Maddie at the elementary school.

A few faces in the crowd are familiar. I recognize the ones who teach or work at Notre Dame, the university where Mom is a professor of computer science in the College of Engineering. I also see star reporters from the South Bend, Indiana, TV news shows. The people I've never seen before are mostly wearing suits and ties.

Mom, of course, is there, in her lab coat, beaming proudly.

"Eggy, why don't you show these folks some of your moves?" she suggests.

"My pleasure," says E.

He moonwalks across the driveway to the garage, where my dad hung a basketball hoop.

"Feed me the b-ball, Sammy," says E. "Bounce me the rock. Distribute the basketball."

Yup. I taught E every bit of basketball slang I know.

I toss him the ball. He twirls around and makes a high-arcing shot.

E snags the ball as it bounces off the backboard, and he lands with a hydraulic, knee-bending *FLOOSH, FLISH, FWUMP.* Then he springs back up, like he has rockets in his heels, and—*WHOOSH... THUNK!*—tomahawk-dunks the ball.

The crowd goes wild.

"But wait, there's more!" says E, sounding like

a late-night TV infomercial. "With Maddie's help, I can also spell all of this week's vocabulary words. For instance, *flutter*. F-L-U-T-T-E-R. Now I will use it in a sentence. 'My butter will flutter over my toast.' Speaking of toast, I can also make toaster tarts for a tasty after-school treat."

You guessed it. Warm pastry topped with swirly icing shoots out of his ears.

"Dr. Hayes," says a roly-poly man with a belly that's about to pop a button on his shirt, "your creation is magnificent."

"Thank you, Mr. Riley."

Oooh. I've heard Mom and Dad talk about Mr. Max Riley at the dinner table before. From what I picked up between bites of mac and cheese, Mr. Riley is a very important, very wealthy graduate of Notre Dame who gives a lot of money to his old school.

I AM DELIGHTED TO SEE ALL MY MONEY BEING PUT TO SUCH GOOD USE. NOW, PERHAPS YOU CAN GIVE THE NOTRE DAME FOOTBALL AND BASKETBALL TEAMS SIMILAR JUMPING TECHNOLOGY?

"As the single-largest contributor to the College of Engineering," Mr. Riley continues, "let me just say that this is a great day for Notre Dame! And, if I may quote legendary author Kurt Vonnegut, 'Science is magic that works.'

"So three cheers for Professor Elizabeth Hayes and her magical robotic creation, E, the substitute student!"

As a dozen people start singing the "cheer, cheer" part of the Notre Dame fight song, E and I climb aboard our bikes.

We pedal away, stirring up a wake of swirling autumn leaves, and E can't resist showing off all sorts of bike stunts he learned when Mom slipped a *BMX-treme* DVD into his internal disk drive.

YOU THINK I'M OVERDOING IT?

LITTLE BIT.

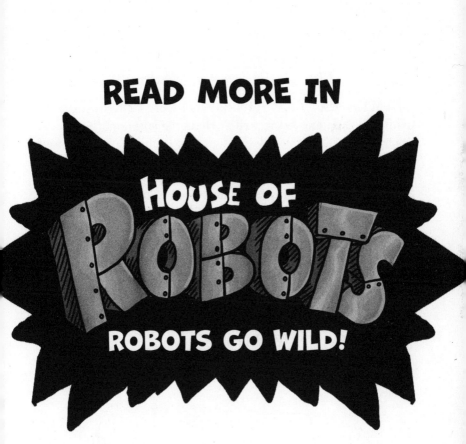

READ MORE IN

HOUSE OF ROBOTS

ROBOTS GO WILD!

JAMES PATTERSON has had more #1 bestsellers for children than any living writer. He is the author of the Middle School, I Funny, Treasure Hunters, and Daniel X novels, as well as *House of Robots* and *Public School Superhero*. His blockbusters for adults, featuring enduring characters like Alex Cross—in addition to his many books for teens, such as the Maximum Ride series—have sold more than 300 million copies worldwide. He lives in Florida.

CHRIS GRABENSTEIN is a *New York Times* bestselling author who has collaborated with James Patterson on the I Funny and Treasure Hunters series, and *House of Robots*. He lives in New York City.

JULIANA NEUFELD is an award-winning illustrator whose drawings can be found in books, on album covers, and in nooks and crannies throughout the Internet. She lives in Toronto.